W9-CIF-823

LORETTA MASON POTTS

by MARY CHASE

pictures by HAROLD BERSON

The New York Review Children's Collection
New York

THIS IS A NEW YORK REVIEW BOOK
PUBLISHED BY THE NEW YORK REVIEW OF BOOKS
435 Hudson Street, New York, NY 10014
www.nyrb.com

Published by arrangement with the
Mary Coyle Chase Literary Trust

Library of Congress Cataloging-in-Publication Data
Chase, Mary, 1907–1981.
Loretta Mason Potts / by Mary Chase.
pages cm. — (New York Review children's collection)
Summary: Ten-year-old Colin Mason, the eldest of four children, learns from a neighbor that he has an ill-behaved older sister who, when he meets her, takes him down a secret tunnel to a fairytale world that seems to connect with many Mason family secrets.
ISBN 978-1-59017-757-0 (hardback)
[1. Fairy tales. 2. Magic—Fiction. 3. Brothers and sisters—Fiction. 4. Adventure and adventurers—Fiction. 5. Secrets—Fiction.] I. Title.
PZ8.C38Lo 2014
[Fic]—dc23
2013050862

ISBN 978-1-59017-757-0
Also available as an electronic book; ISBN 978-1-59017-758-7

Cover design by Louise Fili Ltd.

Printed in the United States on acid-free paper.
1 3 5 7 9 10 8 6 4 2

CONTENTS

To Karl, Toni, Tag and Claire Fanning—the charming children for whom she wrote this story several years ago, the author affectionately dedicates this book.

1. A FACE AT THE WINDOW

Colin Mason was ten years old before he learned he had an older sister. And he never forgot this day—because things were never the same again.

It was on a Saturday morning in late September he found out about her. But there was nothing to tell him that morning when he woke up in his little bedroom under the gables of the big house that this day would be very different from all the other Saturdays he had known.

The woodbine outside, turning crimson in the autumn sun—why didn't it begin to shake and jiggle and whisper to him? "Oh-Oh Colin—you just wait! Today is the day,

Colin—" or else "We know something you don't know!"

Or the yellow bird with the long black tail, sitting on the branch of the locust tree outside his window—why didn't it give him some kind of warning? Pecking at the window, for instance, with his long black beak maybe in a Morse message—dot-dash-dot dash— "trouble ahead, Colin! Operation Loretta!"

But none of these things happened. Colin was to learn as he lived longer that important days often begin like ordinary days.

He woke up as usual, looked lazily about himself, stretched inside the warm clean sheets and wondered what he would do this morning; ride his bike, of course. He always rode his bike. Go see the guys maybe—his friends Whitey Boggs and George Swenson up the street. He liked to play with them.

But this was not always easy. First, he would have to deal with his mother; second, he would have to slip away from his younger brother and his younger sisters.

He heard a sound on the stairs outside. Someone was coming up to his bedroom, step, step, little short steps. That would be his mother.

She was a little woman and, even though she always wore very high spike heels, she was not much taller than Colin himself. He smiled. He would tease her. There was knock, knock, at the door and then her voice.

Loretta Mason Potts

"Colin! Oh Colin! Colin Mason, are you asleep?"

"Yes," he answered, "I am sound asleep. I can't hear you."

"Colin, get up this minute. You have to go to the store for me. We are all out of cornstarch."

A few minutes later, still yawning, Colin parked his bike against the wall of the building and went into the grocery store. He had a dollar bill in his shirt pocket. Standing over by the canned peas he saw two of his mother's friends—Mrs. Moore and Mrs. Newby. Mrs. Moore wore such a tiny hat you could hardly see it and Mrs. Newby wore such a big hat you could hardly see her.

Now Colin could not and would not say one word against these women. But he had already heard everything they had to say. It was always—"My, my what a big boy you're getting to be!"

So he turned and walked over to the place where the fresh vegetables were lying on the racks and he held his finger under the sprays of water dripping on the carrots. It was then he heard it.

Mrs. Moore was saying to Mrs. Newby, "That is Colin. He is the oldest of the Mason children. Isn't he getting to be a big boy?"

He waited for Mrs. Newby to agree and say, "Yes, he is the oldest and yes he is getting to be a big boy."

She did not say this. Instead she said, "Oh no, he is not the oldest. There is another one—an older one. There is Loretta Mason Potts."

At first Colin almost burst out laughing. He started to turn around and say, "That's silly! I'm the oldest. I am—" But he didn't.

There was something, suddenly, which kept him from saying that. And this was a little sound inside Colin's head like a little wind beginning to blow. It blew up many things in his memory; things which had never made any sense before. And he listened to the sound of this little wind and while he listened for it he also heard what else these women were saying over by the canned peas. Mrs. Moore was saying, "My dear Mrs. Newby, you must be out of your mind. I have known Colin's mother for years and I tell you absolutely he is the oldest child in the family."

Mrs. Newby answered, "My dear Mrs. Moore, it is you who are out of your mind. I have known Colin's mother longer than you and I tell you he is not the oldest child in that family. The oldest is this awful, awful, bad, bad, girl—Loretta Mason Potts."

Mrs. Moore's voice grew sweet—too sweet as she asked a question Colin wanted to ask himself.

"And who told you, Mrs. Newby?"

Mrs. Newby laughed a thin little laugh.

"A little bird told me," and she reached for a can of peas and walked over to the cashier, her big hat bobbing like an umbrella.

When Colin got home his mother was combing and brushing the hair of the other children. She stood in the midst of them and she was so small herself that it did not look like a mother standing in the midst of three children. It looked like four children standing together, taking turns combing each other's hair. And you wouldn't have been surprised to hear the mother call out, "Ouch, ouch, stop, you're pulling, you're hurting—let go."

On the left of her stood Kathleen, whose nickname was Kathy. Kathleen had an angel type face. Colin looked at her suspiciously.

Up until this morning he had always thought she was the oldest Mason girl just as he had thought he was the oldest Mason boy. Now he frowned at her. Why hadn't she told him she was not the oldest? So as he walked by her he reached out and gave her a shove.

"Colin, shame on you," his mother cried out, "and you the big brother!"

Colin stood over in a corner and watched her pulling the comb through the short, newly cut hair of his younger brother, Jerry, six years old.

But Jerry Mason did not think of himself as Jerry

Mason or as six years old. He was Jerry, a cowboy, and he rode the range on a big horse. When he was eating oatmeal or sitting in school or sleeping in his little bed he was always riding that big horse across the range—whee! Giddy yap! Giddy yap!

And next to him stood Sharon Louise Mason, five, the youngest one. Colin was sure of this. Maybe he didn't know any more who was the oldest but he did know who was the youngest. It was Sharon.

Sharon was young enough so that she was never lonely. When the other children went to school, people of all shapes and sizes, animals, talking plants and talking chairs, all came out of the wall and played with Sharon.

Now Colin looked at his mother. She was very pretty. Everybody said of her, "That pretty little Mrs. Mason and her four lovely children."

Four children! Colin's eyes got narrow as he looked at her long and closely. Did she know about Loretta Mason Potts?

And his dad! Colin wondered if his dad knew. His dad had left home during the war.

And when Whitey Boggs asked Colin one day, "Which war—the World War or the Korean War?" Colin had told him, "The war between Mom and Dad."

His dad telephoned every Sunday morning from New York. Colin decided to ask him. But now he kept on staring at his mother. He thought if he looked at her long enough and hard enough she would come over to him and say, "Colin, stop staring at me. I will tell you all about her."

But she didn't. Instead she said, "Colin, why are you staring at me like that? Take the cornstarch out to the kitchen."

Cornstarch! He had forgotten to get the cornstarch! His mother was cross.

"You forgot the cornstarch? But that's why I got you up out of bed and sent you to the store. Tell me, why did you forget the cornstarch?"

He wanted to say, "You ask me about cornstarch. Let me ask you something. Am I the oldest in the family? What about Loretta Mason Potts?"

But he didn't. He only shrugged and mumbled something he didn't intend for her to hear and then he went upstairs to his room.

He sat on the edge of his bed. The little wind he had heard in the grocery store began to blow again in his mind.

He remembered the time when they were sitting having dinner in the dining room one winter night. The candles were lit. It was Kathy's birthday. They were waiting for the cake and while they waited they were pushing and shoving each other as people will often do when they wait for the cake.

Kathy was pushing Jerry and Jerry was shoving Sharon and Sharon was pinching Colin and Colin was pulling at Kathy's hair—like a magic circle all around the table—pull, shove, pinch, howl! Then the chorus—"Mother—make him stop. He started it. I did not. Leave me alone."

It was Kathy who looked up and saw it first. She raised her finger and cried out, "Mother—look—at the window!"

"Don't point, Kathy," his mother answered calmly. "Surely one can look without pointing." And then she turned her little head gracefully, half smiling, and looked at the window. The smile faded quickly.

Slowly she laid down her napkin. She got to her feet.

"Children," she said, "there is nothing at the window." Then she walked outside and slammed the door.

The children looked at each other. There had been something at the window of the dining room. They had all seen it. It was a face, a face staring in at them, a face with a nose flattened up against the glass. A face that didn't smile—a girl!

And Mother didn't come back to the dinner table. She came in, put on her mink coat very quietly.

"Cut the cake, Kathy, and a very Happy Birthday!"

Then she had kissed each one of them and gone out.

They had heard the front door slam and her high heels clicking down the steps.

Then there was the time when their maid, Rosalie, had taken him and Kathy downtown to a movie. Passing a big department store he had looked in and seen his mother standing by a counter where they sold nightgowns with long sleeves. Colin had decided to tease her and walk up stealthily behind her and say—something like—"You're arrested! Reach for the sky."

But he didn't. He was too surprised. For he heard her say to the clerk, "I'll take six. This child lives in the country where it is cold on winter nights." What child? But he didn't ask. He didn't say a word to anybody. He ran out of the store and she never knew he had seen her buying six pink and white striped nightgowns for a child in the country.

Then there were the "old coat" nights when Mother would never answer any questions. Every Friday night she came downstairs in the old gray coat and the old gray hat and the shoes with the thick, black soles and the low, flat heels—the ugly shoes. She never put on lipstick and she never wore her rings.

"Are you going to the movies?" Colin would ask.

"No," she would answer, "I am not going to the movies." Then she would always sigh—a deep sad sigh.

Then Kathy would ask, "Are you going to play canasta with Mrs. Moore and Mrs. Newby?"

Mother would sigh again.

"No, I am not going to play canasta with Mrs. Moore or Mrs. Newby. Mrs. Moore is canning fruit and Mrs. Newby is painting china."

Jerry would ask, "Are you going to a big ranch and ride a big horse?"

Mother would smile at him.

"No, dear, go to bed."

Sharon would say, "Take me with you."

"No." Mother would sigh again and say, "Where I am going I cannot take you with me—ever, so please never ask me."

Slam, slam at the door, click click with the heels down the front porch steps and she was gone—into the night. Where, they never knew.

Well, it all added up, Colin decided, as he sat on the edge of his bed that Saturday morning. And when his sisters and brother came into his room, he stood up.

"Shut that door," he told them. Sharon ran over and shut the door hard.

From downstairs his mother's voice came up the stairwell.

"Stop slamming those doors."

"Shh," said Colin, "don't let anybody hear. Come close." They all came close.

Loretta Mason Potts

"You creeps," he began, "you think you are all there is."

Kathy looked at Jerry and Jerry looked at Sharon and they shrugged. What was he talking about? But he hadn't finished.

"We are not all. There is another one, an older one. A bad one. There is a big sister we have never seen. There is Loretta Mason Potts."

They opened their mouths to cry out in surprise, but fiercely he went—shh—shh—

"And what's more, the next time mother puts on that old coat and goes out with those black shoes, I am going to follow her—so shh—shhh!"

2. THE MYSTERIOUS HILL

Colin stood waiting in the darkness at the side of the house. One hand was in his sweater pocket and the other on the handlebars of his bike. His mouth felt dry and his heart was pounding. This was the Friday night he had thought would never come. This was the beginning of the big adventure.

Through the curtains he could see dimly the figures in the house next door moving back and forth. They were Mr. and Mrs. Oliphant. For one second he envied them. They were safe and warm inside their house. Their hearts were not pounding. They knew everybody in their family.

What was keeping his mother? He was waiting there

for her to come out of the front door and hurry down the steps. Wasn't she going tonight? Was this one Friday night she would stay home perhaps? Would he have another week of waiting?

He thought of the past week. Every day had seemed like a longer mile leading up to Friday night. He remembered last Sunday. His dad had called from New York as he did every Sunday. Colin had told him the news of the week, his friends, his school work.

This Sunday Colin had said to him, "Dad, did you know about Loretta Mason Potts?"

Click went the receiver. His dad had hung up on him. Just like that.

On Tuesday Colin had gone up to the attic looking for old pieces of cloth for a tail for his kite. His eye had fallen on a big wooden box. The word "photographs" was written across the top of the box in blue chalk. Colin had walked past it and would never have looked at it twice if he had not happened to see the letters "L—O—" on the edge of one of the photographs sticking out of the side. Then he picked that one up. On the back of it were written the words—

"Loretta—age one year." He had turned it over.

There sat a baby with curly hair and white dress. The dress had lace on the skirt. The baby wore white kid boots.

But that wasn't what made Colin's eyes pop. He rubbed his eyes and looked again. There she was and in her mouth was—a cigarette!

Now the front door slammed. His mother ran down the steps. A taxicab drew up to the curbing. She got in and the cab pulled away like a big yellow pumpkin and glided down the street.

Quickly he got on his bike and started to pedal, but the traffic was heavy. Cars kept darting in and out and once there were so many between him and the cab he couldn't see it. Once a man in a car shouted at him angrily, "Watch out with that bike, bub!" His heart sank. How could he go fast enough to follow mother's taxicab? But something in him made him go on and nothing would have stopped him.

There it was! He could see his mother's gray hat through the back window. The cab had stopped for a red light. He was right behind it now. He lowered his head so, if she should look out, she wouldn't know the boy on the bike was her boy.

Then he had a bit of luck. He heard the cab driver say, "Lady, did you say 4150 Grove Street?"

He heard his mother's voice answer, "No, driver, 4541 Grove Street."

Colin pulled his bike up to the curbing and over it. The automobiles on the boulevard were like boats bobbing up and down in a canal. He saw an empty blue taxi and held up his hand. The driver stopped and eyed him suspiciously.

"You want a cab, kid?"

"Yes," said Colin, "I want to go to 4541 Grove Street."

"What'll you do with the bike?" the cabby asked. Colin didn't answer. He hadn't thought of that.

"Slide it in back behind the bumpers," the cabby told him.

So Colin lifted it. It slipped. He lifted it again and finally it was held in place. He jumped into the cab.

There was no sign of the yellow cab as the blue cab sped down the boulevard. But what difference did it make? He knew the address. Well, the cab driver knew it. He hoped he remembered. Colin didn't.

Once at a traffic light, the cabby turned and said, "You're goin' a long ways out, kid. You got enough money?"

"Oh yes," Colin answered. And he did have. Not with him, of course. But he had a ten-dollar bill at home in a box in his dresser.

Soon they were out of town and out into the country. The roads got bumpy and rutty. Bump! Bump! Bump! The cabby got cross.

"You better fix these roads, kid, if you expect me to come out here."

Colin said nothing.

Then the houses got further and further apart and the moon looked big and silvery across the little farms they passed and even bigger and more silvery across the bigger and bigger farms they were now passing. There was no sign of the other cab.

Then Colin saw a big black hill, rising up, pointed, in the moonlight. One star hung above the point. There was a farmhouse at the bottom of the hill. On a wooden sign at a gate it said: *4541 Grove Street. Orson Potts. Fresh milk.*

The cab slowed up. It stopped.

"Here you are, kid." Colin saw the yellow cab parked a way down the road. He got out.

"Wait a minute." The cabby was opening his door. "That'll be three dollars and fifty cents."

"That's all right," Colin told him, "because I've got a ten dollar bill home in a box in my dresser."

The cabby didn't say anything for a minute. Then he said, "I'll wait for you and we'll go to your house and get it." Then as Colin started to walk through the gate to the farm he called out, "You better come back if you want your bike."

"I'll be back," said Colin, "just as soon as I find out if I've got an older sister."

The house of Orson Potts stood far back from the

road. It looked like a big black teapot. The chimney rising from one side of the roof looked like the spout and the smoke coming out looked like steam.

Behind it stood the black pointed hill and once, just for a second, Colin thought he saw little lights flashing on that hill.

Between the house and the hill stood trees, standing close together like people who might leap out at you like a gang.

"I'm not scared," Colin told himself. "It looks scary but I'm not scared."

He stopped still once as he thought he saw someone run from behind those trees, stand for a moment and then run back. He couldn't see who it was or what it was. But he had the funny feeling that whoever it was had seen him. He took a deep breath and in a minute started walking again.

"It wasn't anything," he told himself, "I just thought it was." Then he heard voices.

He ran toward the sound and found himself looking through a window into a kitchen. He saw his mother sitting at a kitchen table with two other people. One was a tall thin man with a black mustache, bib overalls and a straw hat pushed back on his head. The other was a woman with a checkered apron and a knob of hair twisted on top of her head.

The man was pounding the table with his fist.

"She's gettin' worse, ma'am."

The woman was rocking back and forth in a rocking chair shaking her head mournfully.

"Everything's worse. Heaven help us! Heaven help us!"

His mother looked so sad. She sat at the table with her head bowed. The man said, "The principal of the school is comin' here tonight to talk to us about her. She's gonna git expelled."

His mother raised her head. There were tears on her face.

"Please call Loretta again. I must talk to her. Oh, where is she?"

Colin saw the man walk to a door, open it and then he saw torn wallpaper and a flight of steps leading upstairs. The man bawled loudly, "Gal—you up there? Git down here. Your ma's here."

Then as Colin waited to see at last this awful girl, this bad sister, no one came. The wind got colder and he shivered in his sweater with his eyes glued to that stairway, but nothing happened.

Then Colin heard footsteps at the front porch and then voices. He ran back and hid himself by the side of the porch behind a bush.

He saw a woman with a hat with a bird on it, get out

of a car, walk through the gate and up onto the steps of the porch. This, he decided, must be the principal of Loretta's school. Just as she was about to knock at the door he saw a figure run from the other side of the house up onto the porch. It was a girl.

Colin couldn't see her too clearly even in the moonlight, but he did see that she had long braids of hair hanging down her back. She wore a sweater with a torn sleeve. And he had a strange feeling as he looked at her face. She looked something like Kathy and something like Sharon. Yes, she was certainly his sister. This gave Colin the oddest feeling. It was like going miles away from home and finding the old living-room chair in some stranger's house.

She walked over and stood before the woman.

" 'Lo, Miss Gutshall."

"Well, Loretta! Well, well!" The woman drew herself up, very large and very stern, "Well."

Loretta's voice when she spoke was very sweet and polite.

"A well is a hole in the ground," she said, dropping her head.

"Open the door, Loretta. I came to talk to your folks."

Loretta's head came up slowly.

"I'll open the door, Miss Gutshall, but you can't talk to my folks."

"And why not?"

Here Loretta looked at Miss Gutshall in surprise.

"Didn't you know? Haven't you heard?"

Then she put her arm up before her eyes and her shoulders shook with sobs. Miss Gutshall stretched forth her hand.

"There, there, Loretta. Don't cry. What's the matter?"

Loretta quickly dropped her arm. Colin saw that her face was dry. There were no tears in her eyes.

"They got killed, Miss Gutshall. They're dead. A big truck hit Mr. and Mrs. Potts right out there an hour ago."

Then she pointed with her forefinger to the road and Miss Gutshall's eyes turned and followed slowly.

"No," she gasped, "oh no, not really!"

"Oh yes," insisted Loretta, "right there, by that tree. They were walking slow and the truck was comin' fast—and squash!" Here Loretta brought her hands together in a sharp, hard clap.

"Oh dear," cried Miss Gutshall, "how awful! How terrible!"

Loretta nodded her head.

"There was lots of blood," she said. "I got some on my apron—see!" Then she pointed to a spot on her apron.

Miss Gutshall shook her head back and forth slowly.

"You poor child," she said. "You poor, poor child. So young for so much sorrow. I look at you and my heart aches."

Loretta hung her head. "Yes, ma'am," she answered. Again the tone of her voice was low and shy.

Miss Gutshall looked up at the star over the black pointed hill behind the Potts farm. All the stiffness and starch was gone out of her.

"This is a strange world, child. No one ever knows what will happen. I came out here tonight with my heart full of anger toward you. I was about to expel you from the school again—but forever. And now—and now—"

Here she reached out and patted Loretta's head.

"And now I am full of pity for you. I will come in and use the telephone and call the superintendent."

Loretta took hold of the screen door and held it open for her.

"Shh," she put a finger to her lips. "Come in, but don't step on them. Mother Potts is on the sofa and Father Potts is on the floor."

Miss Gutshall jumped back.

"Never mind," she said, "I'll be back later."

She started to run down the steps. Then she turned.

"Aren't you afraid, dear child, to be out here alone with them?"

Loretta smiled. "Oh no, Miss Gutshall. They look so peaceful."

Miss Gutshall threw her arms around her and hugged her tight.

"You darling child," she wept, "you are so brave. You make me ashamed of myself."

And the last thing she said before she hurried away was a question.

"Loretta, do you have any other relatives? Any brothers or sisters or anybody?"

"No, ma'am," answered Loretta, "I haven't got nobody but that hill back there."

"Poor child, poor child," Miss Gutshall was saying as she hurried to her car.

But Colin saw that as Loretta turned and looked at the hill she was smiling happily.

He stood still as a mouse behind the bush. Then he felt a sudden impulse to jump up, run to her and say, "They're not dead. They're in the kitchen. You must have seen the truck hit somebody else."

But another thought struck him. It made him feel cold.

Was Loretta Mason Potts—his own sister—a big liar? And why didn't she mention Mother? Or him or his brothers and sisters? Didn't she know about them either?

But then he heard Mr. Potts's voice bawl loudly again, "Gal—you out there? Git in here."

But Loretta did not move. Calmly she took a candy

bar out of her sweater pocket and began to munch it slowly.

The door was flung open and there stood his mother and Mr. and Mrs. Potts.

"Loretta," his mother cried out and she rushed forward and threw her arms around the girl. She stroked her hair and made loving, cooing sounds to her, the same kind of sounds she made to him when she was pleased with him, saying things like, "How is mother's own big girl? How is my dear Loretta?"

But Loretta did not even turn her head.

"Hey, don't slop," she said, and she walked away from Mother.

Mr. Potts took hold of her arm. "Who was here?" he asked. "Who was you talkin' to out here?"

"Miss Gutshall," answered Loretta, and she went right on calmly munching the candy.

Mother Potts spoke up. "I knew it, Pa. I told you I heard a car. Where is Miss Gutshall?"

"Gone," sighed Loretta. "All gone—real gone."

"Gone where?" demanded Father Potts. "Where's she gone to?"

Mother Potts said, "She wanted to see us—about you—"

"She came," said Loretta and she said it in the tone of one who is bored with everything, "to beg me to be in the Christmas play. I told her 'yes' and then she went away."

Colin's mother faced Mr. and Mrs. Potts.

"Hear that," she said. "I hope you heard that! This child has talent. She has always had talent. And you tell me the principal wants to expel her! Mr. Potts and Mrs. Potts, I do not understand you."

Mrs. Potts started to answer and her face looked angry. But Mr. Potts held up his forefinger and wiggled it back and forth.

"Keep outta this, Ma. The time has come for a few plain words. We've been keepin' a wildcat and you're tryin' to tell us—it's a lamb!"

Colin's mother raised her head high in the air like a queen. Her voice became low and steady and she took hold of the gold bracelet on her wrist and began to turn it slowly round and round. This always meant she was very, very angry. Not just a few minutes angry but a long-time angry.

"Mr. Potts," she said and looked up at him, "and I believe your name is Potts. You know nothing about anything. This child is not a wildcat. Wildcats live in trees. They have green eyes and crafty, mean dispositions and no one would dream of inviting one of them to be in a Christmas play." She put an arm around Loretta and stood close to her, "So you see, you do not have a leg to stand on."

Mr. Potts took out his pipe. Slowly he filled it from a little white sack in his shirt pocket. He lit it and he puffed at it before he spoke again.

"Ma'am, supposin' we leave Christmas plays clean outta this discussion. There is no connection between a Christmas play and this rascally ornery daughter of yours."

"Good for you, Pa," said Mrs. Potts and she went over and stood close beside him, "don't take no back talk."

"Keep outta this, Ma," he answered, but he stayed close to her just the same, just as though they had chosen up sides and it was he and she against Loretta and Colin's mother. And all the while the moon was shining down on the little rickety wooden porch. The wind was cold and Colin felt the ground cold under him as he crouched and listened.

The only thing that was warm was the anger of the grown people on the porch. But Loretta did not look angry. She only kept on munching the candy bar and looking away from them. She kept looking at the black pointed hill beyond the Potts farm. There was a secret kind of smile on her face.

"Let's take you back a few years, ma'am," said Mr. Potts, now putting his thumbs inside the armholes of his bib overalls, "when you brought this gal out here for the first time. Remember that?"

Mother tossed her head. "Why talk about that? Loretta was only a baby then, five years old."

Mr. Potts shook his head.

"That one was never a baby. She mighta been young but she was never a baby. From the day she set foot in this house she was a full-grown rascal and a devil."

"High-spirited, Mr. Potts," answered his mother, and she stroked Loretta's hair. "She was high-spirited and that was all."

But Mr. Potts was not finished.

"She ran off to play in the woods on that hill while you was buyin' a gallon of milk and you could hardly get her to leave this place. I had to help you get her into the car and she was kickin' and screamin' like a wildcat. You took her home and she wouldn't eat or sleep. You brought her back the next day and begged us to help you."

Mother's voice had changed. Now it was sad.

"Yes," she said, "and as soon as I drove through that gate with her she stopped crying and when she came into your kitchen she ate a piece of bread and smiled. I was heartbroken. It was either have the child starve at home or live out here with you."

Mr. Potts laughed an ugly laugh.

"The fat was in the fire from that day on. Whenever you tried to take her home she kicked and screamed again."

Mother sighed.

"What happened to her, Mr. Potts—Mrs. Potts? What happened to her that first day that made her want to leave her own home and mother and live out here with you?"

Colin saw his mother wipe tears out of her eyes with her handkerchief. He wanted to run up on the porch and put his arms around her. And he was so surprised! Loretta had not been sent away because she was bad. She had *wanted* to leave home and live on this rickety little old dairy farm. Why?

His mother was asking Loretta the same question.

"Loretta—for the hundredth time—please tell Mother what happened to you that day to turn you against your own family and toward Mr. and Mrs. Potts?"

But the same secret slow smile was on Loretta's face and she did not look at his mother and she did not answer. She looked beyond the Potts farm toward that pointed hill. Colin's eyes followed hers but he saw nothing but the same black hill, sharp and pointed in the moonlight with the one star hanging above the point.

"Seven years." Mr. Potts nodded. "This wildcat has had us in hot water seven years!"

Mother did not hear. She was thinking out loud.

"I was ashamed for the neighbors to know, for my other children to know that my own child had turned against me and preferred the milkman."

"Seven years and three months, Orson," said Mrs.

Potts, "and that's too long."

Mother nodded.

"Yes. And I now see that I made a horrible mistake in ever bringing her back here to you. Tonight has proved it to me. The stories you have been telling me about her are not true. You said she was to be expelled from school but instead they want her to be in a Christmas play."

His mother's voice grew dangerously sweet. "What's the matter, Mr. Potts? Are you jealous? Didn't anyone ever ask you to be in a Christmas play?"

Before he could answer mother went on.

"I have been wrong all these years to doubt my child and believe your lies. Well, Mr. Potts, it is finished. Give me your bill and I will take her home with me—tonight!"

Colin's heart turned to ice.

Bring her home! Oh no! Couldn't his mother tell that it was she who had told the lie? He felt like rushing up on that porch and telling her the truth. Then he saw a strange thing. He saw Loretta walk over and stand between Mr. and Mrs. Potts. She had chosen up sides.

"Get away," cried Mrs. Potts. "Oh Pa, what if we starve. I'd rather starve than have her."

Loretta spoke but she did not move away from them.

"Oh, don't starve," she said, and she handed something to Mrs. Potts.

"See how sweet she is," cried Mother, "she would give you her candy. Come, dear, let's get your things and we will go home and you will be with your mother and your brothers and sisters."

But Loretta did not move.

Colin looked at what she had handed Mrs. Potts. It was the paper wrapping off her candy bar. Sweet? How could his mother say that?

Mrs. Potts began to nibble absent-mindedly at the paper. Then she spit it out.

"I shoulda known better," she said. "Go on, gal, get your clothes and go along home with your mother." Then she gave her a shove.

Loretta still did not move.

Colin's mother walked over and pulled her.

"Come, dear," she said, "you don't have to stay with these people who tell lies about you. Come home with your mother."

But Loretta jerked her hand away from mother and stepped closer to Mr. and Mrs. Potts.

He shoved her away. "Git goin'," he said, "we don't want you here."

But each time he shoved her toward mother, Loretta would step back toward him.

Mother shook her head sadly.

"See how sweet she is. No matter how you've treated her, she still loves you."

Mr. Potts laughed an ugly little laugh and puffed on his pipe. "Loves us—ha—ha—ha! Hear that, Ma?"

"Loves us," echoed Mrs. Potts, "loves us, my foot! Look at my nose. Once it used to be in the middle of my face. But she nailed my shoes to the floor one day when I was taking a nap in my rocking chair. When I got up I pitched forward—like a sack of meal. Loves us—ha—ha!"

Mother's face turned pale.

"Oh, don't tell me she doesn't love you! Why would she refuse to eat until I brought her back to you? Why did she turn against me and her own family if she didn't love you?"

Mr. Potts laughed again, this time uglier and longer.

"She don't love nothin' but that hill back thar, ma'am. If she could take that hill with her she'd go home with you. Ain't that so?"

And he shook Loretta's arm as he said this. "Ain't it—ain't it?"

Loretta was still smiling the sly, secret smile.

"Like as not," she said.

Mother was so puzzled. She turned now and looked at the hill. "She loves that hill! How could anyone love a hill? It looks black and sharp and cold."

Then she looked again. "What are those lights flickering up on that hill, Mr. Potts?"

"I don't know, ma'am. That's a mighty strange place up there. I wouldn't walk up that hill if you paid me. But her—" and here he turned to Loretta, "that's where she runs to all the time. That's why she wanted to come out here—not for me—and Ma—but for that hill."

Mother said, "Nonsense. Why would a child leave her own home for an ugly, cheerless thing like a hill? Come, Loretta!"

But Loretta did not move toward Mother. Instead she made a move toward the house. But Mr. Potts grabbed her and held her tight.

"She's fixin' to run up on that hill again. No, you don't, gal. You git home with your mother and stay there."

Mother said, "Loretta, you have no choice. Mr. and Mrs. Potts do not want you. You've got to come home with me."

And with Mr. Potts holding her and mother pleading with tears in her eyes, Loretta did an odd thing.

She put her thumbs in both ears and wiggled her fingers.

"Why is she doing that?" asked Mother.

"She means Elkhorn," said Mrs. Potts, "that's the orphanage down the road a piece."

Mother's voice got angry.

"Loretta, take your thumbs out of your ears. You cannot go to an orphans' home. Not when you've got a home of your own. Are you trying to break my heart?"

Loretta lifted her eyes and for the first time looked into her mother's face.

"Oh no, ma'am," she answered simply, but she did not come toward mother.

"We'll have to pick her up and carry her," said Mr. Potts. "You take hold of her head and me and Ma'll git holt of her feet."

But Loretta broke and ran. Colin saw Mr. Potts reach out and catch her. Loretta fastened her fingers around the post of the porch and hung on for dear life while she looked back at the hill.

For one second Colin thought he did hear a sound like tinkling, tinkling music coming from that hill. But the next second he decided it was the night wind blowing through the pine trees.

And all the while Loretta was hanging onto the post. She was screaming now as Mother and Mr. and Mrs. Potts tried to pull her away.

"Let go," she was yelling, "turn loose off'n me."

"It was just like this seven years ago when I tried to take her home," said Mother as she breathed hard and tried to keep hold of the struggling girl.

"She's bigger now," grunted Mr. Potts, "and she kicks more, ma'am. You better git that cab driver to come in here and help us."

The Mysterious Hill

Colin saw his mother run toward the yellow cab parked out on the road. Then he kept close to the bushes and stealthily ran out of the gate and jumped quickly into the blue cab.

"Hurry," he told the cab driver, "don't let anybody see us." And as the motor roared and the blue cab started back to town he looked out of the window and saw his mother and the other cab driver running toward the porch of the Potts farm.

He could still hear Loretta screaming– "Turn loose offa me. Let go–let go–darn you."

And he was saying in his heart as the cab sped along the bumpy rutty roads, "Hold on, Loretta. Don't let go. Don't go home to our house, Loretta Mason Potts."

But nevertheless even with this fear in him he could not help wondering what *was* up on that hill?

3. A BAD GIRL COMES HOME

It was early the next morning. The house was full of breakfast noises and breakfast odors. From the kitchen, where Rosalie, the maid, was busy, there drifted the smell of coffee percolating on the kitchen stove, going "aah—erp—erp—ahh—erp—ahh—erp." There was the smell of hot toast and melting butter and syrup and pancakes.

Outside there was the sound of cars carrying people to work downtown; of milk trucks clattering along the pavement. Across the tablecloth in the dining room was a broad ray of pale breakfast sunshine, which looks entirely different from lunchtime sunshine.

But this morning Kathy and Sharon and Jerry were

not seated at their places at the table. They were standing beside the empty chair which had been placed right next to Mother's chair.

As soon as Colin walked in and saw that empty chair he knew the worst had happened. They had pried her loose! Loretta Mason Potts was in this house!

Kathy pointed to it. "Who's that for?"

Colin frowned. "Skip it," he said.

"I'll skip it," Kathy answered, "but who's it for?"

"Somebody slept in the guest room," said Jerry.

"We've got company," said Sharon.

Now they could hear Mother's high heels coming down the stairs. They were going "click, click" as always, but there was another sound this morning, too. Other feet were coming downstairs with her. The children quickly sat down in their places and sat up straight as poles.

"Good morning, children."

They turned. There was Mother, smiling happily, and beside her stood a girl almost as tall as she was. This girl had two long braids of hair, and she wore a blue sweater with a hole in the sleeve. Her dress was gray cotton. It was wrinkled. Her hands were not clean.

But just the same Mother was standing close to her and had her arm around her!

Kathy wanted to cry out. "Mother, don't hug that

dirty girl!" But she didn't. She sat still and wondered.

Jerry wanted to say, "Gee—who's that?" and Sharon felt like going over and pulling Mother's arm away from her.

Colin only glanced at her and then turned away. Had she seen him last night? He could not tell from her face. She did not look at any of them. She looked cross and bored.

"Children, stand up." Mother smiled. They pushed their chairs back and stood up.

"This is your sister."

"Sister!" they echoed. That is, all of them except Colin.

"Loretta Mason Potts," Mother patted her shoulder, "but it's not Potts any more. She has come home to live with us—at last."

Live with them! They were so surprised their mouths fell open. Then they smiled. "A new sister! What fun!"

But Colin did not smile. He knew better.

"Colin," his mother was calling him, "come here and meet your sister, Loretta. Loretta, this is Colin. He is a fine boy. He is my right arm. He gets A in everything."

Loretta stared at him so long and hard that Colin was sure she had seen him last night and would say so now. But she didn't. Instead she nodded her head slowly.

"He can walk by his self, too," she said.

"Walk by his self"—but of course! He was ten years old. What a silly thing to say!

Mother did not think so. She nodded and smiled.

"You were learning to walk when Loretta went away, Colin. Sit down. Kathy, come here."

Kathy came forward. And because she was a girl she put a smile on her face and her voice was polite and cheery.

"Good morning, Loretta. I'm Kathy."

Loretta looked at her closely, too.

"She looks different with hair."

Different with hair! Kathy was puzzled. Mother explained.

"You were a bald-headed baby in your cradle when Loretta went away. Loretta, these are the little ones. They were born after you left. Come, Jerry! Come Sharon!"

Jerry was the first. "Gosh," he said, "I didn't know you were *my* sister and why did you go away?"

"Shhh," frowned Mother. "It's not polite to ask personal questions. Sit down."

Sharon took her turn. She walked to Loretta slowly, her arms folded behind her back, her red and white dress hiked up, showing her little white petticoat with the lace edge. She looked like a dear little old-fashioned child on a dear little old-fashioned valentine. And she said to Loretta, "You sock me and I'll sock you."

Loretta's head came up quickly and she looked respectfully into Sharon's eyes.

Mother said, "Go back to your chair, Sharon. Please excuse your little sister, Loretta. She is very young. She will get over it."

Mother smiled so happily. "My family of children, all together at last." She hugged Loretta. "Look around here, dear. Do you remember this house, this room?"

Loretta answered without looking. "Nope" she said.

"Nope," the children echoed. "Nope?" and they looked at Mother.

"Shh—" answered Mother, "that's Potts talk. We will get all of the Potts out of Loretta's vocabulary in a few days."

They all sat down at the breakfast table. The children were shocked as they saw that Loretta leaned both elbows on the table and yawned twice without covering her mouth with her hand. But despite this, Mother was happily filling her plate first, heaping it high with toast and pancakes and jam.

Loretta pushed the plate away. "Don't want no grub." And she yawned again. "I ain't hungry."

Mother's smile faded. She jumped up from the table.

"Scrambled eggs," she said, "I'll get you some scrambled eggs." And she hurried to the kitchen.

As soon as the kitchen door was closed, Loretta looked at all of them and said, "I won't eat no eggs. And I'm not stayin' here. I'm goin' back to the Potts farm—as soon as I get a streetcar slug."

Colin felt in his pocket. He had the money left over from the ten-dollar bill he had changed to pay the cab driver last night. His fingers found a quarter. He decided it was worth it.

"Here," he handed it to her. "Take this."

Loretta grabbed the quarter and jumped up from the table and started to run quickly to the front door.

"Loretta," cried Kathy, "don't go."

But Colin made a face at her. He lowered his voice so they could hear him and Loretta couldn't.

"Shh—let her go. She's a crum," he said.

So they said nothing. But just then Mother came back from the kitchen with a plate of eggs.

"Loretta, where are you going?" she asked.

"Nowhere," Loretta answered, and her eyes flashed warningly at the others as she sauntered back to the table. "Ain't goin' nowhere, ma'am."

"Go off to school, children," Mother said. "You can get better acquainted with your big sister when you get home this afternoon."

Loretta said nothing, but she thought to herself, "This afternoon. I won't be here this afternoon. I'll be back at the Potts farm, back on the hill, and as soon as she turns her back I'll run out that door."

When Mother saw that Loretta was not eating the scrambled eggs, she thought to herself, "It isn't eggs she needs. This child needs love and new clothes and pretty presents." And out loud she said, "Loretta, come upstairs with me. I want you to see your own room. Rosalie has been airing it out for you. I have tried to keep it nice, always hoping you would come home someday."

And Loretta thought as she followed her meekly upstairs, "I will only wait until she turns her back and then I will run."

But she answered, "Yes, ma'am," and followed her meekly upstairs.

As they passed one room in the upstairs hallway, Loretta stopped and stared in amazement. Sitting in that bedroom, on a little wooden rocking chair, was the most beautiful little creature! She had long golden hair, turned under at the ends like a page boy's. Her dress was yellow tulle with little rosebuds and made like a ballet dancer's skirt. On her feet were red satin dancing slippers.

Loretta did not mean to, but she cried out— "Oh! Oh!"

"That is your sister Kathy's very best doll," explained Mother. "And her name is Irene Irene Lavene."

There was a shelf like a bookshelf on the wall of this room. In each cubbyhole was a doll. There were small dolls, thin dolls, baby dolls, lady dolls, man dolls, boy dolls, old woman dolls. Everywhere Loretta looked there were dolls, dolls, dolls. It looked like a store full of dolls.

Each doll was in perfect condition. There was none without shoes or stockings; none sitting in a slip with her dress rumpled in a heap in the corner; none with hair half combed or half washed; none with wigs off; none smeared with jam or crayon or ink. Each doll was fresh and smart looking.

Mother explained. "Kathy takes such good care of her dolls. She allows no one to play with them but herself, and when she plays she plays very quietly. She comes up here for an hour each day after school. Mondays she plays with the babies, on Tuesday with the ladies, on Wednesday with the men, Thursday with the boys, Friday she dusts the shelves, Saturday she changes the places where they sit, and on Sunday—every Sunday morning—she plays for two hours with Irene Irene Lavene."

All Loretta could say was, "Well." She could not take her eyes off Irene Irene Lavene. She knew suddenly that she had to have that doll. She could not and would not leave this house without her. She wanted her more than she had ever wanted anything—except

Potts hill. And she told herself then that she would take her there and show her to—Them.

Mother had to pull her gently out of the room.

They passed Colin's room full of skates, mechanical toys and footballs, but Loretta did not even glance inside. They passed Jerry's room full of space helmets and guns; Sharon's room with a few dolls all helter-skelter, wigs off, dresses off, shoes off, lots of crayons and paint books. But Loretta did not look.

Now they were at the room at the end of the hallway. Mother took a key out of her pocket.

"I have never allowed the others to come in here, dear," she said. "I have kept it—just for you. It is your old room."

It was a beautiful little room. It had a small brown wooden bed with a bright red bedspread. There was a big white dog with black shoebutton eyes embroidered on the spread. At the windows there were white ruffled organdy curtains, tied with red organdy sashes like perky bows on a party dress. On the floor was a soft yellow rug. There was a little white fireplace at one end of the room with brass candlesticks and yellow candles. There was a little desk in the corner and a chair, cushioned in cloth with red and yellow flowers. It was all so charming!

But Loretta was not looking at it. She was seeing, instead, a room with a shelf and beautiful dolls, but most of all a big doll in a dancer's costume, named Irene Irene Lavene.

Mother's hand touched her arm. "Do you like it, dear?"

Loretta made circles on the yellow rug with the toe of her old brown shoe. There was a sly look in her eyes.

"I like it," she said, "but I don't need it. It's too nice for me. Give it"—and here she raised her head and looked into her mother's eyes, "to someone who needs it. Just let me sleep anywhere—on the floor or the back porch maybe."

"Oh, Loretta," and tears came into Mother's eyes, "don't say those things. I want you to have everything you want and be happy here."

Loretta walked to the window and looked out at the big maple trees on the lawn. "Well," she spoke slowly, "you could just give me that dirty, nasty little old room, that one back there."

Mother was puzzled. "Kathy's room?"

"Give this nice one to her," said Loretta.

"Oh, Loretta," Mother said, "you want your sister to have the nicest room!" She walked close to her and hugged her. "We can't do that to you. Her room is too small for you."

Again the sly look crept into Loretta's eyes. "But it's

closer to your room, ma'am."

Mother's eyes again filled with tears. "Of course, dear. You have been away from me so long. Very well, I'll have Rosalie move Kathy in here and we'll take your things in there. And now we will go down town and buy you some new dresses."

Loretta smiled to herself. It had been so easy. Things were so easy if you just knew how. She would be in that room with Irene Irene Lavene, and tonight when they were all asleep she would get up and dress and take that beautiful doll and run for the streetcar—back to the Potts farm—back to the hill—back to Them!

4. THE SINGING DOLL

The first place Mother took Loretta was the fourth floor of Skimmerhorn's Department Store—the beauty shop. It smelled of soap and water, perfume, hair oil, manicure oil. On the walls were pictures of movie stars; movie stars with hair cut long and flowing, long and curly, short and curly or short and straight like Italian boys. Mother asked for Mister Louis.

"Mister Louis," she said, and smiled at the little man in the white coat with the big scissors in his hand. "This is my daughter, Loretta."

Mister Louis was the kind of man who, when you told him something, said right away it was not so. So now he looked at Loretta with her wrinkled gray dress, her long braids and scuffed shoes, and he said, "This is not your daughter, Mrs. Mason!"

"Yes," said Mother proudly, "she is my daughter and we are going to have her hair cut. So figure out, please, a nice hairdo for a twelve-year-old girl."

Mister Louis lifted Loretta's long braids. "It is a serious problem" he murmured, and then for a moment he forgot where he was and thought he was driving a horse—a horse and buggy. He cried out, "Giddy up—giddy yap—whoa!"

Loretta did not care for Mister Louis. She pointed to a picture of a beautiful blond movie star who had a page-boy cut, softly turned under at the ends. Who did it look like? Irene Irene Lavene, of course. "I'll have one like that," she said.

Mister Louis dropped her braids. "Whoa," he said, "you are not the page-boy type. Better for you a nice little guzz-guzz here and a kind of oop-de-doop feather edge there."

"I'll have that," said Loretta and pointed again to the picture.

Mister Louis said "Whoa" again.

But Mother said, "Let her have what she wants, Mister Louis. She has been away so long."

When they left the beauty shop, Loretta had a soft page-boy cut and soft bangs. She looked better, but she did not look like Irene Irene Lavene.

The next stop was the "Junior Miss" dresses on the sixth floor. Mother looked through a rack of nice cotton dresses and navy blue serge suits with trim little jackets and skirts with kick pleats. "Which one do you like, Loretta?"

Loretta looked everywhere but she did not see anything she liked. "These cost too much. Just get me a little yellow dress with yellow lace up to here."

"But that's a ballet dancer's costume, Loretta. You could not wear that to school."

"I don't have to go to school, ma'am. I can stay home with you and do the dishes."

"You dear child," Mother sighed, "you dear, dear child. Just for that I will get you two of everything."

So when they took the elevator to go downstairs, Loretta was wearing a little blue serge coat and a little blue serge suit with a white collar, and on her head was a small straw hat with blue ribbon streamers down the back. On her feet were shiny new black patent-leather slippers. Mother looked at her and beamed with pride.

"You look so nice, Loretta. I am so proud of you."

Loretta dropped her eyes. "You look nice too, ma'am, and so does your mink coat."

Mother did wish Loretta would call her "Mother" and not always "ma'am," but she decided that would come in time.

They stopped in the fountain room downstairs. There were glass cases filled with white cakes, chocolate cakes, caramel cakes and strawberry cakes. Waitresses were carrying trays of butterscotch and ice-cream sundaes, fudge sundaes and ice-cream sodas.

"I'll have a chocolate ice-cream soda," Mother told the waitress. "What will you have, Loretta?"

Loretta suddenly remembered something Mr. Potts was always saying. She said it now. "It's a hard thing to earn a dollar. Just bring me a glass of water."

Mother smiled softly. "Thoughtful child," she murmured to the waitress. "Bring her a double chocolate ice-cream soda."

The next stop was the office of the principal of the Aaron Heinkerberger Junior High School.

"Miss Jennings," Mother pushed Loretta forward, "this is my daughter Loretta, who has been away from us for so long. I want you to enroll her."

Loretta was startled. She did not know what the word "enroll" meant. It sounded as though she was going to be thrown down on the floor and rolled over by a steam roller into something flat and thin.

So she said, "Ma'am, I don't care to be enrolled." Then she pointed at Miss Jennings. "Enroll her," she said, "if you want to enroll somebody."

Miss Jennings looked puzzled as she heard Mother introduce Loretta as her daughter, but she decided not to ask questions. "Loretta Mason, age twelve. We will put her into section six. Send her tomorrow promptly at eight-thirty, sharp."

"Ha—ha," thought Loretta as they walked out, "tomorrow I will not be here. I will be out on the Potts farm and I will have my new clothes and Irene Irene Lavene and I will show her to—*Them!*"

She was getting impatient. She wanted to return home now and sprint up those stairs into that room and kneel down by that doll.

But Mother had more plans. "We must go to Penny's and get you new underwear and then we will stop at the jewelry store and buy you a nice little wrist watch so you can tell time."

Loretta said, "But I don't want a watch, ma'am. I can tell time. When it snows, it's wintertime, and when it's hot, it's summertime. So why spend money?"

But Mother insisted and they bought a tiny little gold wrist watch just the same.

Downtown they met one of Mother's friends, Mrs. Moore, who looked *so* surprised when Mother introduced Loretta as her oldest daughter.

Mrs. Moore smiled, however, and said, "Hello, Loretta."

Loretta said, "Good-bye, Mrs. Moore!"

When Mrs. Moore walked away, Mother whispered, "When you are introduced to people, Loretta, you say 'hello,' you do not say 'good-bye.' "

Loretta thought this over. "It saves time, ma'am," she said "and you want me to save time, don't you? You bought me this watch!"

5. THE SECRET TUNNEL

At last they were home. Before Mother had the key out of the front door, Loretta was half-way up the stairs. She stood still one second before the door of her room—or Kathy's room—and enjoyed a delicious moment of waiting, the kind just before you bite into a piece of candy.

Then she opened the door slowly, closing her eyes as she stepped inside, and then she opened them. She could not believe it!

Was she in the wrong room? Oh, no, because on the wall paper there were still the marks where the shelves had stood. And in the corner on the rug the marks where the little rocking chair had sat. But there was no shelf full of dolls. More than that! There was no Irene

Irene Lavene! She let out a cry.

Mother ran into the room. "Loretta, what's the matter? Did something frighten you?"

"She's gone," gasped Loretta. "She's gone."

"But of course she's gone. She is Kathy's doll, and Rosalie moved all of Kathy's things to the other room—to your room. Loretta!" Mother looked at her in surprise. "You didn't think Irene Irene Lavene went with this room, did you?" And that was what Loretta had thought. But she didn't say that.

"Irene, Irene?" She made her eyes get big and wide, "Gosh, who's that? I meant my little sister, Kathy."

It was a few minutes before dinner. Mother and all of the children except Loretta were sitting in the living room. The house felt warm and cozy. There was the smell of roast beef and gravy and mashed potatoes drifting from the kitchen.

Colin was stretched out on the sofa. Kathy was lying on the floor reading a book. Sharon was coloring a color book with crayons. Jerry had one leg over the arm of one big chair and he was halfheartedly clicking his gun.

Mother laid aside the evening paper. "Children, while your sister, Loretta, is upstairs hanging up her new clothes I want to speak to you. Colin, sit up. Kathy, stop reading. Jerry, stop clicking. Sharon, stop coloring."

There was silence. Mother's face was so serious. Her eyes were misty.

"Your sister, Loretta, is a wonderful girl. I was wrong ever to believe anything else. I will never again trust anyone by the name of Potts. Loretta is sweet, unselfish, affectionate and thinks of saving money. She is starved for love. I want each and every one of you to be nice to her—always—nicer than you have ever been to anybody before."

The children exchanged uncomfortable glances. They waited for Colin to speak. He did.

"Who's hurting her?" he asked.

Jerry aimed his gun at the green vase on the table and went "Bang—bang."

"She better leave my guns alone. If she does, okay. If she don't, bang, bang, bang—dead."

Kathy's face was puzzled. "Why can't I have a new blue suit, too?"

Mother frowned. "Shame on you, Kathy! You have beautiful clothes and Loretta's clothes are old and torn. You have twenty-five dolls and she has none. Poor girl."

Kathy thought this over. "I will let her play with one of my boy dolls sometime."

Mother kissed her. "You are a sweet girl, Kathy. That will make her very happy."

"Next Christmas maybe," Kathy added, "for a few minutes before church."

It was bedtime, nighttime. The house was dark. Every

bedroom door was closed. Outside the wind blew through the maple trees with a swishing swooshing sound.

Mother, lying in her bed, often said to herself at night, "It sounds like wind and water outside. What if this house turned into a ship during the night? What if it were to rise up from the ground and sail off through the skies—on and on—forever and ever?"

But always at this thought she would say, "Oh no, ship, not yet. Don't sail yet. Not until *everyone* I love best is on board with me."

And here she would always sigh, thinking of her oldest daughter, Loretta.

But not so tonight. Loretta was on board tonight, too. So Mother heard the wind outside in the trees and she smiled happily. "Lift up the house—let it sail through the skies—in and out among the stars—on and on—forever and ever! At last tonight, everybody I love best is on board with me—so ship ahoy!" Then she fell asleep with a little smile on her face.

But Loretta in her bedroom was not sleeping. She was looking at the wall where the dolls had been and she was looking longest at the marks in the rug where Irene Irene Lavene's little rocking chair used to be.

She listened. Hearing nothing now, she got out of bed, hurried over to the clothes closet, put on her new shoes and her little blue serge suit and felt in the pocket for her quarter. She opened the door of the room quietly and hurried down the hall to Kathy's room. The door opened easily. Kathy was sound asleep with her head buried in the pillow. The smaller dolls were all sitting quietly in their little cubicles on the shelf. And there, patiently waiting, sitting upright in her little rocking chair in the moonlight, sat Irene Irene Lavene.

Loretta got down on her knees beside the doll. Almost fearfully she touched the soft yellow hair and felt the yellow satin dress. She patted the little red satin slippers with the cunning crisscross ankle straps. She breathed deeply in adoration. Oh Irene Irene Lavene!

Would they charge for her on the bus? She would hold her on her lap. And on the long ride out to the Potts farm she would talk to her. She would take off the little red satin slippers and put them on again. She would hold her across her arms and let her go to sleep. Then she would wake her up and sit her up again. She had never in her life seen anything quite so beautiful. She had never wanted anything so much.

Gently she slid her hands under the outstretched arms of the doll, the arms which seemed to be saying to her, "Take me—take me." Gently she lifted her up.

Then it happened. From nowhere a sweet little voice began to sing:

"Don't ever leave me, sweetheart. If you do
I'll surely die.

Don't ever leave me, darling, or the tears
will fill my eye."

Light flooded the room. There was a scream! Kathy was sitting up in her bed, her eyes wild. Doors opened down the hall. There was the sound of running feet. There was Mother's shocked voice calling, "Kathy, Kathy, what's the matter?" Mother stood in the doorway in her blue velvet wrapper, looking frightened.

Colin and Jerry and Sharon stood behind her. All fastened their eyes on Loretta.

Now there are two kinds of people in the world. There are the kind who, when they hear a strange noise, drop whatever they are holding and let it crash. Then, there are people who grab on tighter than ever. Loretta was this type of person. So she held Irene Irene tighter than ever and the voice still sang:

"Please tell me, dearest playmate, that
we will never part.
O pick me up and hold me close or you
will break my heart."

Then there was a silence and then a little whirring, whirring sound like a mechanical toy running down.

Kathy jumped out of bed and ran sobbing to her mother.

"Mother, Mother, she was trying to take Irene Irene Lavene."

Mother smoothed her hair. Then she picked her up, big as she was, and carried her back to bed. She took Irene from Loretta's arms and set her back down in her own little rocking chair. Then she moved the chair over beside Kathy's bed. Mother's face was stern. "Loretta, come here to me."

"Yes, ma'am," Loretta said and she walked primly over to Mother's side and stood close beside her. She stood so close to her she almost knocked her down. She stood on Mother's feet.

"Not that close," said Mother and she moved a step away so she could lift up Loretta's chin between thumb and forefinger and look into her eyes.

"Listen to this. A long time ago your daddy saved a man's life in the war. This man was a toymaker. He wanted to make a doll for Kathy. He spent a year making her the finest doll he had ever made. Kathy named her Irene Irene Lavene because she came wearing a ballet dancer's dress and Kathy thought that name sounded like a ballet dancer. There is not another doll in the world like her. She sings when you pick her up and stops singing when you put her down. She can sing sweet songs and torch songs. She can also recite nursery rhymes when you stand her up by the chair and place one arm behind her back."

"What?" and here Loretta gasped with astonishment.

Mother went on. "Whenever you touch her or pick her up she makes sounds. So no one can ever take her without Kathy knowing it. No one in this house ever plays with her except Kathy. We made Kathy a promise we would never touch her. In this house we keep our promises. You must not touch Irene Irene ever again. You hear me?"

But Loretta did not hear her. She had turned her head to look again at Irene. She was more wonderful than she had guessed. Sing songs! Speak pieces! Oh Irene, Irene!

Mother shook her shoulder. "Loretta, Loretta, do you hear me?"

Loretta murmured, "She speaks pieces? Let me hear her speak a piece."

But Mother's voice was rising. "Certainly not! It's late. And why aren't you in your nightgown? Loretta, do you hear me?"

Colin, standing in the doorway, wondered what was wrong with his mother. Couldn't she see that Loretta was not listening to her. And couldn't she see that with every word she said about Irene Irene, Loretta looked harder at the doll and the little glint in her eyes got bigger and bigger like a bonfire growing and growing and crackling?

He watched Loretta as she finally raised her bonfire

eyes to her mother and said softly, "Oh, yes ma'am."

"That's fine," Mother answered and patted Loretta's head. "That's my good girl. Now go to bed and take off those clothes—and get into your nightgown. Everybody go back to bed."

Loretta walked quickly out of the door and into the hall and they all heard the door of her bedroom slam.

Mother smiled at Kathy. "Go to sleep, Kathy. Your sister just did not understand. Now she understands and we will have no more trouble."

Colin walked slowly to his room. Was it possible his mother had believed Loretta? He didn't believe her. Oh well, maybe he was wrong. Mother knew best.

Loretta, in her nightgown, sat on the edge of her bed and wondered what to do. She had to get back to the hill in back of the Potts farm—to Them! And she had to take Irene Irene with her. But how?

As she sat puzzling she heard something. It was the faint sound of tinkling, tinkling music. Her eyes flashed. She jumped up. Her breath came faster.

"Them! It's Them! It's Their music!"

She ran to the window. There was nothing out there. She looked behind the dresser. There was nothing there. She even looked under the rug on the floor. Nothing there!

Then she saw a flash of light from under the door of

the clothes closet. She ran over and opened it. Now there was a big flash of light and now the music was louder!

Mother's voice came down the hall. "Loretta, Loretta! Why are you out of bed. I'm coming down there!"

Loretta closed the closet door and ran to her door.

"Don't come, ma'am. I'll come to your room. I'm coming. I'm coming." She ran out looking back all the while at the closet door.

Colin heard strange sounds of music and sat upright in his bed. He listened again and heard nothing. Then as he was about to lie down again he knew he did hear something. He got out of bed and went down the hall to Loretta's room. Yes, there was funny music in there.

He opened the door. The room was dark but there was a ray of light from underneath the clothes closet door. He walked over to it and opened the door. He gasped at what he saw.

The wall at the back of the closet was swinging open—like a door—and through this door in the wall he saw a lighted tunnel!

"Gosh." He rubbed his eyes. What was it? Where did it go?

He stepped inside the closet. He saw that the tunnel was dug down, down into the earth and little lights were strung along it—stretching far, far down, as far as his eye could see.

The first thing he knew he was running into that tunnel and his bare feet were going slap-slap as the walls of the tunnel echoed and echoed and echoed!

6. THE ASTONISHING CASTLE

Colin didn't know how long he had been running through that tunnel. It seemed to him that it went on and on and on for miles and miles and miles. But never once did he think of turning back. And just as he thought it would never end, it did end and he found himself running out of it into a forest!

There were so many trees! Before him there was a small path cut through the trees. Gosh! Then he heard something. It sounded like—tinkling tinkling music again. Then it stopped. He heard water running. It sounded like a hose left running at night but it was a bigger sound than that. He felt the ground cold under his bare feet. He reached out and touched one of the trees. The bark felt rough under his hand. He looked around in amazement.

There was a black pointed hill rising up into the sky! Where was he? He looked down and at the foot of the hill he saw the lights of a farmhouse. The Potts farm! The Potts hill! Loretta's hill!

He saw what looked like smoke. It was mist rising from a little stream and there was a stone bridge across the stream. He put out his hand and touched the stone railing of the bridge! He had to make sure he wasn't dreaming. It was very cold. Listen! There was that tinkling music again!

As he crossed the bridge he felt the strangest sensation, a melting, dizzy feeling like a merry-go-round, or like the sudden drop of an elevator in a tall building.

Suddenly the feeling stopped. And Colin's eyes popped open at what he saw now. He was over the bridge and looking up at a great lighted house. Before him curved a wide stairway of stone, curving round and round and up and up.

The staircase looked as if it was striped black and white, like a zebra, but that was because of the lights and shadows which fell across it. There were tall trees planted at the edge of it, and the shadows of the trees fell across the steps, except where the white light of the moon lay between them.

He crept up those steps, one black step, one white step, and at the top were the warm yellow lights of the rooms inside that big house.

He saw a great metal door with a lion's head on it. That was the knocker.

Now he was looking through the curtains into a richly furnished room. There was a fire burning merrily in a fireplace, soft white rugs on the floors, little gilt tables, sofas and chairs upholstered in rose and blue velvet. But there was not one person in that room.

The little tables had silver coffeepots and cups and saucers stacked beside them. The room looked as though it were waiting for a party. Sometimes he could hear music. Sometimes he couldn't.

Oh! Didn't that fire look good and that white rug look soft! His feet were so cold and he was shivering in his pajamas and bathrobe. The window was open. So he threw one leg over the sill, felt the warm white rug under one bare foot. With his heart beating he climbed all the way inside. There was no one here! Softly he hurried over to the fireplace and warmed his hands, held out first one foot and then the other, all the time watching the door across the room, a big double door painted in white and gold.

The music seemed to be coming from there. Whenever it stopped he heard the clapping of many hands.

Then it would begin again. He looked up.

From the ceiling hung crystal chandeliers, sparkling like dewdrops in the sun. In a corner, there was a gold piano.

"Gee," he thought, "a gold piano. Who owns this house?"

But at that moment, he saw the doors opening and he ran quickly and hid behind the velvet drapery at the window. Now many people came pouring into the room. They were all dressed in party clothes. The ladies were wearing lace and satin gowns in many colors. The men were wearing black suits with long tails and white shirt fronts.

They were all laughing and talking and buzzing like a swarm of bees. One woman in a blue lace dress with a long gold chain went over to the gold piano and began to play. A man in a red and white uniform with gold things at his shoulder went over to turn the pages of the music for her. He had a sword at his side and when he bowed the sword stuck out behind and it looked like a rooster bending down to pick up corn in a barnyard.

The ladies sat on the little sofas, poured coffee into the cups and handed them gracefully to the gentlemen. It was a big party in a big rich house. But whose house?

It must be, Colin decided, the house of Mrs. Alfred Van Hummelwhite. He had never seen it but he had heard his mother say it was the richest house in town. His mother had been there to a party once and she had told them there was a fountain and a pool in the middle of a room where fish swam. He would like to see this pool before he left here.

Just then the lady with the gold chain stopped playing the piano. She stood up and raised one hand. The buzzing noise stopped. The ladies handing the cups, held them in the air. The gentlemen reaching for them stopped with their fingers outstretched—very still.

"General," she spoke to the man with the sword, "and ladies and gentlemen. I feel there is a stranger here."

The ladies and gentlemen jumped to their feet. A murmur of voices rose. "A stranger here—where?"

The man with the sword—the General—now raised his hand.

"Please," he said. Then he pulled the glittering sword from its sheath. "The Countess must be informed immediately. The ladies will kindly withdraw. The gentlemen will follow me."

Led by the woman in the blue dress the ladies ran across the room and through the double white doors. The gentlemen lined up behind the General, and Colin saw them all walk to the velvet draperies of a window across the room. He saw the General place one white-gloved hand on one hip and hold the sword low. He heard him cry out as he faced the velvet curtain, "Rascal! Come forth on the count of three. One—two—three—en garde!"

Then he lunged forward, plunged the sword into the velvet drapery and withdrew it and held it high and glittering. "What! No blood! He is not there!"

Then he went to the next window and did and said the same things at the next drapery.

Colin's heart pounded in excitement as he watched. And he felt a little wave of disappointment each time the General held forth the gleaming sword and cried, "No blood."

The procession moved around the room. It was not until they were only three windows away from him that Colin realized they were looking for him!

He wanted to run out of the draperies and cry out, "Stop! I'm Colin Mason and my mother knows Mrs. Van Hummelwhite. So put up your sword." But he found he could not move. His legs might have been made of lead. His tongue was stuck to the roof of his mouth and his backbone felt like water. They were so close now he could see the little wrinkles around the General's fierce blue eyes and he could even see the faces on the medals he wore on his chest. He could hear him breathe and hear his knees creak as he lunged forward. And just as Colin thought that he would be run through with the sword surely, he saw the General stop moving. The heads of the gentlemen turned. Colin heard a clang, clang noise outside and saw the ladies running in excitement out of the ballroom, their silk dresses rustling.

"She," said the General, "is at the door. Our tunnel is a successful piece of engineering. Bravo!"

Then Colin saw the most surprising sight he had seen in this long night of surprises. He saw his sister, Loretta Mason Potts, walk into the room in her nightgown and her old sweater with the torn sleeve and at the sight of her he saw the most radiant smiles come over the faces of all the grand and beautiful people in this rich and beautiful room. The women cried out in joy and the gentlemen bowed from the waist. The General sheathed his sword.

"It's Loretta," they cried and rushed forward. "Tell the Countess it's Loretta."

They all crowded around her with excited little cries. The ladies patted her shoulders. The gentlemen beamed and smiled at her tenderly. For a moment there was such a crowd around her Colin could not see her. Then he saw her push her way rudely through them.

"Stop pawing," she said, "and go get lost."

Colin felt ashamed. How ashamed his mother would be if she could see one of her children talking so rudely at

Mrs. Van Hummelwhite's party! He waited to see the faces frown and the smiles fade.

To his surprise they all laughed in great delight. "How refreshing," they cried. "Get lost! But how utterly, utterly amusing!"

The General bowed over Loretta's hand. "You are never dull," he said. "Let me escort you to a chair."

And he took her by the hand as though she had been a great and beautiful lady, wearing satin, and not a long white nightgown and an old sweater with a hole in the elbow, and he led her to the prettiest sofa of all, close to the fireplace, and sat her beside the table which had the most silver trays with the fanciest cakes.

As he saw Loretta reach forth a grubby hand for one of the cakes, Colin sighed with relief. Bad as she was, she had managed to save him. They had stopped the search. But he sighed too soon. The lady in the blue dress with the gold chain spoke again. "General, I still feel there is a stranger here." But the General did not hear her.

"My friends," and he drew himself up very straight, "the Countess approaches."

Everybody got to their feet—even his sister, Loretta Mason Potts.

The big double doors were flung open and the music played softly as into the room walked, very slowly, the most beautiful creature Colin had ever seen. She did not walk but seemed to float. And you knew when you watched her that nothing in the world could make her hurry—not even a flame of fire pursuing her.

Her hair was gold and glistened under the chandeliers, first dull gold, then bright gold. Her dress was red satin, made of so many tiny ruffles that between steps it looked smooth and when she moved again it broke into little ripples like the tiny ripples on a pond. On her feet were red satin slippers with diamond buckles and her face—her face was so beautiful—it looked among all of the other faces like a bright star dropped from the heavens, sparkling on dull, brown earth.

It wasn't only that her eyes were so big and blue and the lashes so long and black or her skin so soft and white, it was that her whole face seemed to say something. No matter what words came out of her mouth, you didn't hear them because always her face said the same thing. It said, "How wonderful you are! How long I have waited for you!" And it said this to Colin, hiding behind the velvet curtains.

He wanted to run out and cry, "Here I am. It's me. Look! Look!"

Surely the toymaker who had made Irene Irene Lavene had seen this face in a dream and tried to copy it. But he had failed.

The Countess was much more beautiful than Irene Irene Lavene. And now she was floating ever so gracefully over to where Loretta stood. She put out a white hand and smoothed Loretta's new page-boy bob.

"My dear child," she said and smiled tenderly, "how I have missed you! You have not been here since night before last." Then she took Loretta's hand and led her to another sofa, just big enough for two, and Colin wished she had taken his hand. She smoothed a place beside her on the sofa for Loretta to sit and Colin wished she had been smoothing this place for him. Then she waved the lacy little fan in her hand around Loretta's head gently, gently, and she drew her head onto her own shoulder and said, "There, there there."

Loretta laid her head on the Countess's shoulder, and for the first time Colin saw his sister look happy.

The General spoke. "We greeted her, Countess, and she said, 'Stop pawing me. Get lost.' "

The Countess threw back her head and laughed a silvery, tinkling laugh. "How very amusing!" She waved her little fan. "How utterly, utterly refreshing!"

And all of them laughed gaily again as Loretta grinned and kicked her feet back and forth.

Then the Countess made a little signal and the ladies sat down as close to Loretta and the Countess as they could get. The gentlemen stood.

"Tell us," said the Countess, "about these strange people who tried to steal you away from us and our castle on the hill."

"Well," began Loretta, "there are four of them. Colin and Kathy and Jerry and Sharon."

"Write down those names, General," ordered the Countess, and the General took a little pad from his pocket and with a little gold pencil he wrote down the names.

"The first one again, please?"

"The oldest boy is named Colin," said Loretta, "and he gets A in everything."

The Countess fanned herself. "How dull," she said. Dull? Colin felt a wave of shame pass over him.

"The next one," continued Loretta, as she munched a cake, "is Kathy, short for Kathleen, and she hangs up her clothes every night and she's quite a little lady."

The Countess yawned, "What a bore!"

"The next one," said Loretta, "is Jerry, and he plays with guns all the time."

The Countess sat upright. "He does." Her eyes sparkled. "How fascinating!"

"Oh, they're not real guns. They're only play guns," Loretta explained.

The General bristled. "Not real guns!" His face grew red, "Surely, Countess, you do not insist I write the name of this—this impostor in my personal book."

"Of course not, General," the Countess laughed, "Don't be absurd. Go on."

"The youngest is named Sharon and when she met me she said, 'If you sock me—I'll sock you.' "

"Delightful," said the Countess. "Do put that name in your book, General. I like it."

"Now who else?" she asked Loretta. "Isn't there someone else?"

"No," said Loretta. "That's all."

The Countess took her hand. "I seem to feel there is someone else."

Loretta dropped her eyes. "Well, there's Mother."

"Yes," the Countess exchanged a look with the others, and then she put her hand under Loretta's chin, "and what about her?"

"Well," Loretta finally spoke, but her voice was low and she had trouble getting out the words. "She looks after the children—and well—that's all I guess."

"Oh, no," and the Countess smoothed Loretta's hair again, "I feel there is something more to it."

"Well," and here Loretta sat upright, "she said I couldn't play with that doll. That I could never play with that doll."

The Countess yawned. "How ordinary of her! How very dull!"

"She said," and here Loretta seemed to be arguing with herself, "that she'd promised Kathy and people should always keep promises."

Colin saw everybody throw back their heads and laugh. He saw his sister look odd for a moment and then she laughed, too. The Countess stopped laughing.

"Promises," she said, "when one wants to play with a doll! How boring. Do tell us something amusing, dear child."

Loretta was thinking hard.

"Yesterday in school, the teacher put me in the closet for throwing spitballs. And when I was in there I ate her lunch. She was going to expel me."

There was instantly a loud roar of laughter.

The Countess was laughing so hard she placed a white hand at her red satin side. The General was guffawing so loudly he had to hold onto a table. Loretta grinned. The Countess kissed her on the forehead.

"You are so amusing. You are never dull. You are adorable." And she hugged her tight. "We all adore you."

Loretta stopped chewing on her cake. Then she turned her head and looked at the Countess. "Nobody likes me but you and your friends. Mr. and Mrs. Potts didn't like me. My brothers and sisters don't like me. And my mother didn't like me—not after Colin and Kathy came."

To his great surprise, Colin saw a tear fall from Loretta's eyes and drop onto her nightgown.

The Countess drew her arm away. She yawned.

"Don't be dull, child," she said, and she frowned. When she frowned all of the others turned aside and frowned and the General put his white-gloved hand to his mouth to stifle a yawn.

"A bit of a bore, all this," he murmured.

Loretta quickly dashed the tear from her eye.

"I'll get that doll," she said. "I'll lie and scheme and do anything. But I'll get that doll."

The Countess stopped yawning and put her arm back around Loretta. The General slapped his thigh and the peals of laughter again rose in the room.

The General came over and bowed over her hand, "May I have the next waltz?"

"No," said Loretta, her eyes on the Countess, "go drown yourself."

And then how they all laughed!

"And now," said the Countess as she buttoned the buttons on Loretta's sweater, "you must go back through our tunnel or you might be missed and they must never, never, never find out about us or that would spoil the fun."

And here there was a warning, icy note in the Countess's voice as she said the words "find out about us."

Colin felt the ice fill the entire room and reach out

even to him and freeze him as he hid behind the draperies.

"I have never told anyone," Loretta said, "and I never will. Not since that very first day I met you when I came with my mother to the Potts farm to buy milk."

"My friends," the Countess turned to the others and said, "do you remember that first day when we saw this adorable child playing in the forest and we stole out from behind the trees to play with her and we whispered to her—'come back—always come back—to us'?"

The General nodded. "She grows more and more amusing in that dull world of dull people she lives in, and who knows what delightful pranks and stories she will have to tell us the next time?"

Here he twisted his little mustache and beamed fondly at Loretta, and bowed from the waist.

"Oh, drop dead," said Loretta.

He bowed again. As he raised himself he smiled. "I was afraid she might say something like 'thank you,' but she is never ordinary. Drop dead! How amusing! How refreshing!"

"Utterly, utterly," agreed the Countess and she whispered something into Loretta's ear.

Colin saw Loretta turn and run out of the door, waving good-bye to them, as they all stood and waved good-bye to her—adoring her. Laughing, they began to move back to the ballroom when Gold Chain again reminded them, "General, you did not finish the search!" But the General was bending toward the Countess and she was smiling up at him as they moved across the floor. They did not hear.

Colin waited until he saw the two big white doors of the ballroom close behind the last gentlemen. Then he came out from behind the draperies and threw one leg over the sill of the window. He heard a noise. He held his breath. He had knocked one of the china cups off the coffee table nearby.

Quickly, he picked up the two pieces of the broken cup, put them into his bathrobe pocket, got over the window sill and ran fast as the wind down the steps and over the little bridge.

Again, as he was running over the bridge, he felt that dizzy merry-go-round feeling in the pit of his stomach. He ran through the trees, found the lighted entrance of the tunnel at the side of the hill, and just before entering it he looked back. He could not see the house!

All he could see were tiny lights flickering like fire-flies. Then he turned and ran fast, with the tunnel echoing the slapping of his feet.

When he came to the other end of the tunnel he had a bad moment of fright. There was a dirt wall. There was no door. But as he felt of the wall, it gave under his fingers and he found himself in a closet with girls' dresses and when he tiptoed out he was in Loretta's bedroom in his own house. He breathed a sigh of relief. Not only was he back home but Loretta was sound asleep and did not hear him as he went across her room, down the hall and into his own room. What a night!

He fell into his bed and as soon as his head hit the pillow he was sound asleep.

7. THE TEN-INCH COUNTESS

Now Colin had run out of the castle just in time, because the Gold Chain lady had heard the noise of the cup. She had summoned them all back into the room. They were hurrying toward the window. All of them except the Countess. She never hurried. She made her way elegantly through the crowd and stood looking down the stone steps and across the bridge.

"You are mistaken, Madame La Pugh" she said, "there does not seem to be anybody but there does seem to be something. See that white object on the other side of the bridge!"

The General ran down the steps. He was back immediately, carrying over his arm a large white cloth. The Countess fingered it.

"Is it a gown?" she asked and she flung her arms wide while the General hung it on her shoulders. It fell down to her waist.

"No, no sleeves," she shrugged, "it must be a tablecloth. Try it on the table." They draped the cloth over a table. It hung down on all sides.

"A tablecloth surely," said the Countess, "of a rather cheap make. It is not chic. Remove it at once."

But the General was examining it with his monocle in his eye. "I doubt if it is a tablecloth" he said. "There is a name embroidered in the corner and tablecloths do not have names embroidered in the corner—even in that stupid world across the bridge."

"Whose name?" asked the Countess.

"Loretta," read the General. "Loretta—in red thread."

The Countess smiled and waved her lacy fan. "Of course. It is the dear child's handkerchief." She smiled at the others.

"We forget," she said, "how very large they are across that bridge."

"And how very vulgar," said Gold Chain, "it is to be so big and clumsy. But to be like us," and here she placed a proud hand at a proud hip, "ten inches high—that is—elegant."

Loretta

The General bowed. "Well spoken, Madame La Pugh, and now Countess, what shall we do with this vulgar object?"

"Put it away at once," she answered "and never let Loretta see it again. She must never, never know that whenever she crosses our bridge she becomes our size. That is our secret, isn't it, my friends?"

Then she walked gracefully back into the ballroom. They all watched her with admiration but only the General spoke.

"Magnificent creature," he murmured. Then he followed her.

Colin had been sleeping for more than an hour. But whatever he was dreaming he could not possibly have been dreaming that now—at this very minute—over the stone bridge, they were talking about him. For Colin had ruined the Countess's evening. And he had managed to ruin it without being there at the time. This is not an easy thing to do and Colin had never been able to do it before.

Many times in the past his mother had said to him, "Colin Mason, you have ruined my whole day. Now take that toolbox out of that chair so Mrs. Moore and Mrs. Newby can sit down and take those wood shavings off the dining-room table so they can have lunch." But to be able to ruin a party while you are sound asleep in your own bed!

The Countess did not suspect her evening had been ruined until she was on her way to bed. The orchestra had stopped playing. The guests had retired for the night and the Countess was climbing her white marble staircase to her blue velvet boudoir, when she heard the ugly noise for the first time. She listened again. "My imagination," she told herself and climbed the staircase.

Walking into her blue velvet boudoir which was like the inside of a blue velvet jewel box, she pressed the switch on the wall and the moon began to shine and the stars came out. The Countess had had her boudoir redecorated last spring and had directed the job herself. She was very proud of the way things had turned out. She was proud of the silver moon and the silver stars which glittered in her ceiling when she pressed the light switch. But now she frowned. She *had* heard something. She listened again. Of course, it must be the switch under her bed. She examined it. Everything *seemed* to be in order.

The Countess's bed was made of silver in the shape of a boat. But when she had her room done over she had had the bed slightly altered, too. Now whenever she climbed into the white satin sheets, she could feel with her fingers under the bed for the new switch, press it and then lie back and enjoy the gently rocking motion of a boat. She could look up at the stars and moon and drift happily off into sleep. It was utterly, utterly charming and she adored it all.

That noise again! There it was. Was her alarm clock out of order? She stopped the boat and jumped out of bed to examine her alarm clock.

The Countess was very proud of this alarm clock. It was her own idea. To her friends who raved about it, she always made light of it. "A trifle," she would say, "an amusing trifle." But secretly she quite adored it. It did not go off with a rude, sudden shrill ring. The Countess despised sudden movement and rudeness, even in alarm clocks. This clock you could set, of course, at night before you went to bed as you would an ordinary alarm clock. But at the time set, instead of a rude ringing, there would come the sounds of birds chirping sweetly, making the sounds of dawn and first light, at eleven in the morning, twelve noon or two in the afternoon.

Tonight she felt the wires on the clock as she set the alarm for noon. She listened to it tick. It seemed to be in order. And yet there was a *ticking* sound from someplace else. She threw open her window and listened. Yes, there it was! It was outside! She picked up the little white house telephone and called the servants' quarters.

"Olaf," she told her butler, "take two of the yardmen and look about the grounds. I swear I hear a strange sound outside. And Olaf, wait, don't hang up yet. Call the General in the east wing and ask him to meet me on the upstairs balcony off the game room."

She hurried to her clothes closet to select the proper costume. She selected a long black velvet cloak with a hood which framed her face becomingly.

By the time she stepped out onto the balcony the General was waiting for her and Olaf was beside him with the yardmen. The General apologized for his appearance. He had not had time to shave. He looked worried. Olaf and the yardmen reported they had been over the bridge. They had kicked and prodded the underbrush by the side of the stream and they had found it lying there.

"It?" asked the Countess coldly. "What?"

Olaf described it. They had not only found it, they had walked around it, measured it and stood upon it.

"It is, Madame," said Olaf, "a big clock lying in the grass with black leather straps on either side of it. One of," and here he dropped his voice, "one of Their wrist watches."

For a moment no one spoke. The air on the balcony was chilly, but the Countess did not shiver because of this. Her cloak was warm. She made her voice sound light and gay, however. "We must have had an uninvited guest this evening."

The General adjusted the white silk muffler above his red velvet dressing gown. "Obviously, Countess. Madame La Pugh kept insisting someone was here this evening—remember?"

"But who?" asked the Countess.

Olaf had more information. They had turned the watch over and on the back they had traced a name engraved in gold.

"What name, Olaf?"

"The name is Colin—"

The Countess was puzzled. "Colin—Colin! Whoever in the world is Colin?"

The General held up a forefinger. "Wait. I may have it in here. It strikes a bell somewhere." Opening the little notebook he read "Colin Mason, age ten. A in everything."

"Loretta's brother! But how did he ever get here? How did he find our tunnel? Did Loretta break her promise to us?"

"More important," said the General, "how much did he learn—about us?"

"Yes," the Countess nodded thoughtfully. "That is what we must find out—at once. And we must use Loretta. She must bring him here without knowing why and then—we must question him—casually, of course."

"Of course," agreed the General. "We must be casual—at first."

The Countess sent Olaf and the yardmen away to push the thing into the stream, until the noise should stop. But as they hurried off the sound went on—tick—tick—tick.

The Countess put her hands to her ears. "It is horrid," she told the General. "I cannot bear it."

"I don't believe," the General escorted her off the balcony, "that with such noise, it can be a very good watch."

The Countess sighed as the General bent over her hand and for the second time wished her a good night.

"It was a good night," she told him, "and it was a lovely party. But this person—Colin Mason—has ruined, utterly, utterly ruined, my whole evening. Good night, General."

She went upstairs to bed.

8. COLIN AND THE COUNTESS

When Colin woke up the next morning the first thing he thought of was a general with a white and red uniform, lunging toward a velvet drapery with a flashing silver sword and calling out, "Rascal! Step forth on the count of three. One—two—three."

That was a crazy dream he had! And oh, yes, Loretta was in it, too.

Let's see, how was she in it? Oh yes, he dreamt he'd found a tunnel in the closet of Loretta's room and a castle across a bridge!

Dig that crazy dream! How crazy can you get?

He jumped out of bed and ran down the hall to the

bathroom to wash, and brush his teeth.

It was when he was washing his hands he saw his watch was gone. He looked in his bedroom, under his bed and in the drawers of his dresser. He had lost it, his good gold watch, his birthday present.

He heard his mother calling him to breakfast. He pulled down his sleeve so she wouldn't see his bare wrist. He'd look for it again after school.

Colin ran downstairs three steps at a time, slid into his chair, smiled at his mother and began to eat his toast.

Everybody was at breakfast except Loretta.

He was eating his second piece of toast when she walked into the dining room.

Mother smiled. "Good morning, Loretta. Children, say good morning to your sister."

They all cried out, "Good morning, Loretta."

Loretta looked at them through sleepy, sullen eyes. "Oh, get lost," she said as she sat down.

The children gasped. Mother turned quickly in surprise.

Loretta reached in front of Jerry and took a piece of toast. She reached for Sharon's milk and brought it over to her own plate.

Sharon cried out, "Give me my milk. Mother, she took my milk."

"Oh, get lost," said Loretta again, brought the glass

to her mouth and drank the milk down in one gulp.

"Mother!" Kathy's voice was shocked. For Mother did nothing and said nothing. She was studying Loretta's face.

Loretta turned boldly to her.

"When we go shopping again, ma'am," she said, "I want a red satin dress with little ruffles and a diamond crown for my hair." Then she picked up a napkin and waved it back and forth like a fan.

Colin's toast fell from his hand. He had seen somebody else wave something around the way Loretta was waving the napkin. But who? The Countess in the dream! Had Loretta had the same dream? Did two people ever dream the same dream? And before he knew it he said, "How amusing! How utterly, utterly refreshing!"

"Colin!" Mother's voice was sharp. "What are you saying?"

Colin did not answer but he felt eyes staring hard and when he raised his head he saw Loretta glaring at him, her mouth hanging open. She got up and ran out of the room.

"Your sister," his mother was explaining to the others, "is not feeling well this morning. It could be her tonsils." Mother left the table and went out to find Loretta.

Colin, now alone with his brother and sisters, made an announcement. "Loretta," he said, "thinks nobody likes her."

Kathy had an answer for this. "Who could like her?"

"Not me," said Jerry.

"Not me," said Sharon.

Colin said nothing.

As Colin ran down the back porch steps on the way to school, Loretta stepped out from behind the ashpit and took a tight hold of his arm.

"Let's hear why you said that?"

"Said what?"

"You know what. Why did you say it?"

"Let go of me."

"I'm not letting go of you till you tell me. I'll twist your arm till you tell me."

"Try it."

When she began to twist his arm, Colin, who was strong, stepped back lightly and she fell to the ground. He ran down the alley laughing.

"Getting all excited about a dream!"

In the house, Mother sat for a long time in her room. She was remembering many things.

What a sweet baby girl Loretta had been! Naughty often, of course, but always loving with Mother and even jealous when Colin and Kathy were babies. Mother remembered how close she had huddled beside her in the car that day, so long ago, when they had driven out to the Potts farm for a gallon of milk.

But after they'd missed her, looked for her for hours, and finally found her in the woods on the hill behind the Potts farm, she had looked so different! There was a sly look in her eyes and a secret smile on her face.

She ran from Mother!

It was, Mother had often thought, as if a spell had been put on her in those woods, like an old storybook. What had she seen in the woods? Whom had she met?

It was only after that day that people, Mr. and Mrs. Potts, teachers and neighbors, had begun to call her a "bad, bad girl."

Nevertheless, Mother had always begged her to come home. And each time she would smile that sly secret smile and say, "No thank you, ma'am."

"Oh, well," thought Mother, "somewhere inside of her there is still the dear child who sat so close beside me in the car that day. Love is what she needs. I will give her more and more and more and someday my Loretta will really come back to me with all of her heart."

The afternoon of the next day, Rosalie, the maid, was putting clean laundry into the drawers of Colin's dresser as he came home from school.

"Say, Mister." She grinned at him. "Since when did you stop bein' a boy and turn into a little girl?"

"Since never," and he began looking for his jackknife so he could whittle himself a wooden sword.

She followed him and held out her hand. "It's a pretty little thing," she said. She was holding a tiny, tiny little white and blue teacup, a dollhouse teacup.

He shrugged. "It's not mine. I never saw it before."

"It was broken in two," said Rosalie, "but I glued it together. Just look at those teeny, teeny blue roses painted on the inside of this little cup. Looks like they're hand-painted. But what hand could be so small, it could get inside a cup this teeny and paint these here teeny roses?"

"Don't ask me." Colin turned away and kept on looking for his jackknife. "I don't know a thing about it."

But Rosalie would not go away. "If you don't know anything about it, what was it doing in your bathrobe pocket?"

He turned. "My bathrobe pocket? Me, me! have a dollhouse teacup in my bathrobe pocket? Somebody's crazy!"

Rosalie started out of the room. "It must belong to Kathy. I'll put it in her dollhouse."

As he heard Rosalie going downstairs there was one tiny second when that little wind of memory began to blow in his mind again and he thought he remembered something. But it was not a big enough wind this time to blow up any pictures and so he forgot about it—for a while!

He forgot the dream of the castle, too, until the next afternoon after school when Loretta walked into his room with a frown on her face.

He was sitting on the edge of his bed tying on his tennis shoes. She spoke in a whisper.

"Listen, you're supposed to come with me."

"Where? Come where?"

"Oh, someplace." She looked mysterious. "Someplace where you'll get sandwiches and cake and lots of things."

"Not a chance," Colin said. "I'm playing indoor baseball with my friends, Whitey Boggs and George Swenson."

Loretta hesitated before she spoke aloud these words—words she had never spoken aloud before to anyone.

"The Countess said last night for you to come and so did the General."

Colin stopped tying his shoes. "What?" he gasped. "But that's only a dream!"

"It's no dream," she said earnestly. "So come on with me."

He got up and followed her into her room, watched her walk into the closet and push against the wall.

There was the tunnel!

The forest was cool and green. The mist was rising from the little stream as Colin and Loretta stepped onto the stone bridge.

Loretta was used to this bridge. She was used to the strange feeling which always came over her when she walked across it, that swirling dizzy feeling in her stomach.

Once she had asked the Countess about it. The Countess had said, "It must have been something you ate." If it was, then she was always eating the wrong thing, because it always happened about the middle of the bridge. You felt as if you were falling through a trap door. And it was only after the trap door part that she could see the castle at all and the Countess and the General waiting for her always on the steps.

And here they were today, as always, waving and smiling. And as always when the Countess saw her, she ran down the stone stairs happily to meet her. Even though she knew you were coming, you had promised her you would come and you had no other place to go, she would say so gently, so kindly, "You didn't forget me! You did come. Oh thank you. Bless you."

So today as the Countess came running down the stairs, Loretta got ready for these dear, familiar words. And she heard them, too. But as she spoke them the Countess was looking at—Colin! Loretta thought there must be a mistake. The sun must be in the Countess's eyes. So she coughed and said "Here I am, Countess."

The Countess did not hear her. She was gazing so

tenderly at Colin. And her eyes as she looked at him spoke, too. They said, "But how wonderful you are! How long I have waited for you."

"Gee, thanks," said Colin.

The Countess clapped her hands and turned to the General.

"Did you hear *that,* General? He said— 'Gee, thanks.' Isn't that delightful?"

"Magnificent." The General nodded. He picked up Colin's hand and shook it heartily. "Wit," he smiled at him, "wit and dash along with it. A pleasure, old boy, a real pleasure."

When they did turn and speak to Loretta their smiles were as warm and wonderful as ever. But it was not the same. Something terrible had happened!

Once on the playgrounds Loretta had been hit in the head with a big indoor baseball—thud! This was worse. But she said nothing as she followed Colin and the Countess and the General up the stairs. Instead, she tried to walk closer than ever by the Countess's side.

Colin's face was beaming with happiness. Gosh, they liked him! He felt wonderful.

Now they were all having tea in the Countess's little library. An autumn breeze billowed the curtains. It fanned the flames on the candles in silver candlesticks on the tea table. Before Colin was a plate piled high with the best things he had ever tasted: sandwiches with cheese, nuts, chicken; cakes with whipped cream and cherries. As he lifted a cake to his mouth, the Countess, who did not seem to mind that his hands were dirty, leaned forward. "Do tell me about yourself," she said. "You fascinate me."

"Great chap." The General slapped him on the back. "Would you care to try on my sword?" He stood up, unbuckled it and handed it to Colin.

"Try it on," the Countess urged, "I should adore to see you try it on."

Colin's heart pounded with happiness. It was too big, of course, but he could hold it around him just the same.

"Can I—" he patted the white leather sheath—"take it out?"

"By all means," said the General, "and please do."

The sword itself was like a shaft of winter sunlight, bright and cold. The hilt was dull gold and made in the shape of a woman's head, and when you held it in your hand your fingers felt her neck. It was light as a feather and the point was sharp as pain.

Colin cried out, "En garde," and he lunged forward.

"Oh, look out," said Loretta sullenly, "watch what you're doing."

"Shhh—" The Countess held up her little white hand.

"Bravo," cried the General.

"Stunning," murmured the Countess as she sipped her tea. "Such poise! Such style! See, General, how beautifully he throws back his head?"

"This lad," said the General, "is a swordsman of the old school—a poet of the blade."

Loretta went out of the room and slammed the door. No one noticed. Colin was so proud and so happy! "Well," he began, "I can do it better than that. I did it better yesterday. Yesterday I ripped all of the silk curtains at our house. I went like this—" He lunged forward again.

"Stout fella," said the General, "stout, stout fella."

"Of course," Colin added, "I got in trouble at home over it."

"Chin up," the General said. "Trouble to a swordsman is meat and drink."

"My allowance was taken away and I won't get to ride my bike for a week."

The General helped himself to a cake. "Never cared for a bicycle, myself." He turned to the Countess. "Stupid vehicle—you agree, my dear?"

She smiled at Colin. "A bicycle for you? Oh no. You should have a long, low red sports model convertible with your name emblazoned—not painted, but emblazoned—on the door. Much, much, more your style and you do have style. And by the way," here she looked at the General meaningfully, "you should also have a watch, a fine gold watch with your name engraved on the back."

"I did have." Colin stopped lunging. "But I lost it."

There was silence for a moment.

"Where," asked the General, "where did you lost it—I mean—lose it?"

"At school, I think," said Colin. "In the gym, I think."

"Oh." The Countess smiled, and she looked relieved. "What a pity!"

The General smiled at her. Obviously the boy knew nothing. Everybody was happy. It was a lovely afternoon. Colin was thinking that never in his life had he had such a good time. And the minute he noticed his happiness he was sorry he had remarked it even in his thoughts. Maybe you should never notice when you are so happy. Because suddenly it changed after he had his third cup of tea. He chanced to say something. What made him say it, he never knew. He looked at his teacup and said, "My sister has a teacup like this, only it is a tiny, tiny cup."

There was a silence. It got so quiet in that room, you could hear the candle flames sputtering. You could almost hear the air. When Colin raised his eyes from the little blue roses in the bottom of the teacup, the Countess was looking at him. Her eyes were cold. They had hard little points glittering in them, like the point on the sword. The General was frowning, and his hand was on his sword! Colin, suddenly, felt as cold as he had felt warm before. What had happened? What had he said? What had he done? He sat very still.

After endless minutes, the Countess spoke. "What did you say?" she asked in a low voice.

Colin gulped. "Nothing. I didn't say nothing."

The General pushed back his chair and jumped to his feet. The Countess put her hand on his arm. "One moment, General." She turned to Colin again.

"You said something about a—teacup."

Colin leaned back in relief. "Oh, that," he tried to laugh. "I said my sister had one like this in her doll-house. But it's not really like this. It's only a teeny, teeny teacup."

"Your sister, Loretta?" prompted the Countess.

"No, my sister Kathy," Colin said.

Loretta walked back into the room. She went right to Colin.

"It's late. We got to go back."

"Back!" Here in this beautiful room where he was treated like a man—a brave and bold swordsman and a type for a sports car, Colin had forgotten all about home. The Countess gave him her hand.

"Dear Colin," she said, "it's been delightful—completely and utterly delightful. I shall never forget it."

"Yeah," he answered, "it's been—well—it's been—okay."

"You must promise me something." Her voice was pleading with him. "You must come again—on Thursday, at four—promise!"

"Sure," he said, "I'll try to make it."

The Countess watched him run down the stone steps where Loretta was waiting for him at the bridge. She called out to him, "Colin!" He turned. "Do bring Kathy!"

"Bring Kathy?" He was so surprised! He never brought Kathy anywhere. She was his *sister*.

"Yes." The Countess had not finished. "Bring Kathy. We would adore to meet her and please, please ask her to bring her little teacup."

On the way home, across the bridge and all through the tunnel, Colin talked happily.

Loretta said nothing. She had walked across the bridge this afternoon, a girl named Loretta Mason Potts. But that girl had dropped into the stream and vanished. Now as she looked around the forest she didn't say anything out loud. But she asked the trees a question, "Isn't there anything, anyone, anywhere, for me, just for me and no one else?"

But the trees did not answer her. The mist rising

from the stream did not answer her. Nothing answered her.

9. COLIN WANTS A JAGUAR

It was two days later that Colin got in trouble.

"Colin," the teacher's voice spoke to him sharply in class. "Your mind is not on arithmetic. Where is it?"

He did not hear her. He was not in arithmetic class. He was standing in a room in a castle, a beautiful sword in his hand.

"Colin!" she said again but he did not hear her.

"Colin," she said for the third time and this time very sharply.

He jumped to his feet. "En garde," he cried out and lunged forward.

He heard loud laughter. He turned and saw that he

wasn't in a castle. He was in school. There was no beautiful Countess clapping her hands in admiration, crying out, "Bravo! Oh such style!"

There was the teacher frowning at him; the children laughing at him. In his hand was not a sword—but a ruler!

"I don't believe you are feeling well," said the teacher. "You had better go home and lie down and I will telephone your mother."

Colin walked home slowly. This afternoon he walked home past the drugstore because he wanted to buy some comic books.

The clerk pointed to the stack of comic books he had selected and said, "That will be two dollars and forty-five cents, please."

"Charge it to my mother, Mrs. Mason, 805 Gaylord Street," Colin answered and turned to walk out.

But the clerk who had long arms, reached over the counter and took the comic books from Colin's hands. "Your mother," he turned his back to put them again on the rack, "said none of you kids were to charge any more comic books at this store."

So when Colin came out of the drugstore, he was not a happy person. The sky seemed to be a dreary blue and the long cement walk stretching before him to the corner seemed as if it would never end. What a world! No fun!

Then he had an idea. He walked back into the store and slid onto the leather seat of the stool before the soda fountain.

"What'll it be?" asked the same clerk.

"A double chocolate ice-cream soda."

But the clerk did not pick up an empty glass, spoon in the ice cream and then press the squirter. He laid an open palm on the marble counter. "Let's have a look at your money."

Colin decided to let him look at it. He dug into his pants pocket and brought forth a ball of string, a knife and two pennies.

"No soap," said the clerk, which Colin thought was a silly thing to say. He wasn't buying soap.

"Come back when you've got a quarter," said the clerk.

"Charge it to my mother, Mrs. Mason, 805 Gaylord Street."

The clerk nodded, but did not smile. "805 Gaylord Street! I see she hasn't moved since you were in here a minute ago. She told us not to charge any more ice-cream sodas ordered by any of you kids."

Now when Colin got outside on the street this time he felt twice as unhappy. He couldn't decide whether to go down and get on a train or get on a big boat or go out to the airport and get on an airplane. Since he couldn't decide, he started to walk home.

It was halfway up the block he saw it. It was lying like a ship at dock. It was red and shiny as a cherry. The tires were snow white and the nickel shone like silver. It was brand new. The seats were red leather.

"Jaguar!" Colin was so excited he was talking to himself. "A sports convertible Jaguar! What a nervous deal!"

He looked through the window. The instruments on the dash board sparkled like jewels. Had They—had They—left it for him? Oh, boy! Life was good again! He opened the door and slid inside.

He did not see the police car come cruising down the block.

Mother could not believe her eyes a half-hour later when two uniformed policemen walked up on her porch with Colin between them.

"Keep this boy outta cars that don't belong to him," they told her. Then they turned and went back to the cruise car.

But some of the neighbors were watching.

Mother was so shocked she could hardly speak.

"Colin," she said finally, "what does this mean? There must be some explanation."

Colin gave her one.

"I am the type for a long, low red convertible sports car," he told her, "so why don't you sell my bike and get me one."

If Mother could hardly speak before it was twice as hard now for her to get the words out of her throat.

"It's more my style," Colin explained further, "and I do have style, great style. They both said that."

Mother was able to use her voice.

"They?" she asked quietly. "Who are *they?*"

Colin saw that he had gone too far.

"Nobody," he answered, "nobody at all."

"I should think not," said Mother, and her face was getting red. "And how dare you be brought home by policemen and then ask me to buy you a sports car when for two days you have missed all of your arithmetic problems?"

She held up two papers, one marked twenty-five and the other marked zero. "What's happened to your schoolwork? You used to get A in everything."

"Really," said Colin, "how dull of me!"

Mother's voice was sad when she spoke again.

"You will go upstairs now and study and you will study every afternoon from now on until your grades are good again."

Colin started up the stairs. Pretty dull stuff this. Oh, well, there was a place where he was treated like a man.

And only three more days until he went back there. He guessed he could stick this out until then.

Mother watched him go upstairs.

What had happened to Colin? There was a sly, secret kind of look in his eyes. She had seen that same look some place before. Loretta! Yes, Loretta!

And even as she thought this, Loretta came over to her and handed her a piece of paper. It was an arithmetic paper. In green crayon, it said, "D-minus," and then it said, "shows improvement."

Any other time Mother would have smiled. Today she didn't. She was still thinking about Colin.

"That's fine, dear," she murmured as she handed it back to Loretta; "it says, 'shows improvement.' "

"I know it," Loretta answered, "I saw it. I'm the one gave it to you."

"So you are." Mother nodded. "I'm proud of you, Loretta."

"I'm proud of you too, ma'am," Loretta said.

On Thursday at ten minutes of four, Colin and Kathy finally found Loretta. She was sitting alone on the steps of the back porch. She was watching squirrels in the maple tree.

"Well," said Colin.

"A well is a hole in the ground," she told him without turning her head.

"Come on." He was so anxious. "Let's get going—you know where."

"So," said Loretta, "so what?" But she came.

With Colin telling Kathy to "wait and see and shh," they ran quickly up the stairs to her room, Loretta following slowly behind, kicking at the steps of the stairs.

Kathy got frightened when she saw the tunnel behind the clothes closet wall and even more frightened when Colin pulled her across that funny part of the bridge. She turned here and started to run back.

Colin caught her. "Cream puff," he said. "Come on." He couldn't understand why the Countess had insisted he bring Kathy. Loretta understood it still less. Slowly Kathy walked the rest of the way over the bridge and when she saw the big beautiful stone house she forgot everything else.

Kathy could hardly believe her eyes when the Countess ran down the steps crying, "General, they're here. They're here. You're Kathy," she cried, "and you did come. You didn't forget me. Thank you. Bless you. And Colin—and Loretta. How kind of you to remember." The Countess pressed Colin's hand.

Remember? Colin had thought of nothing else. He had thought of it the last thing when he went to bed at night, all day long and the first thing when he woke up in the morning. But he didn't say this. He said, "Oh, that's all right."

The General was bowing over Kathy's hand. "Ravishing—beautiful," he murmured.

Kathy was too surprised to speak. A general, with a sword, bowing over her hand, treating her like a grown-up woman. She tried to act like a grown-up woman. "Oh, thank you," she said, "Thank you very much."

The General turned to the Countess, "Countess, did you hear that? She said, 'Thank you.' "

"I heard it." The Countess smiled. "She is charming, utterly, utterly charming." The Countess touched the string of green beads at Kathy's neck, "She should be wearing real pearls."

There was a cry of pain from Loretta. The Countess ran to her, "Loretta, Loretta, dear child, what's wrong?"

"Let go," cried Loretta, "let go of me—it's my foot. I broke my foot." And she held one foot in the air and hopped around with her face twisted up and her eyes closed.

The Countess called the General. "Poor, dear child" she said. "General, you must carry her up the steps."

"Of course, of course" he said, and he picked Loretta up.

She moaned as he carried her in his arms up the steps while the others ran behind. At the top step he put her down gently.

"Better now?" he asked her.

"I can't tell yet," Loretta said, "but I almost died."

Today they had tea in the Countess's blue velvet boudoir. Colin did not care to try the boat bed because he noticed the General stood aside and watched all of this with a little smile on his face. But Kathy tried it. She could hardly bear to get out of it. "Do it again," she kept crying. "Turn it on again." She was enchanted with everything. Again and again the Countess had to set the alarm and they all listened to the sound of birds chirping.

Colin was amused at first. But after a while he got tired of this. He stood beside the General and when the General winked at him and said, "Women, these women!" Colin wanted to say something which fit the occasion. He finally thought of it. "The world is full of them."

"You are so right," said the General. "That was very well put, old man."

Kathy fingered the ruffles on the Countess's white lace dress. The Countess said, "You should wear white. White is so—so you."

"Look out," cried Loretta, "look out for my sore foot." But no one heard her. The General was speaking to the Countess in a low tone. She nodded.

"When the time is right," she answered him in the same low tone.

Tea was brought in. Today the tea was a chocolate

drink in tall glasses with whipped cream on top. The cakes were baked with butterscotch and walnut fillings. The Countess and the General exchanged a look which seemed to say; "Now—now is the time."

Kathy was speaking. "I always liked white." She kicked happily at the table leg. "I had a white sweater last winter, but a boy named George Swenson chased me and I fell down and it got ripped."

The General turned to Colin. "Did he die on the spot or was it a flesh wound?"

Colin sat upright in his chair. "What?" he asked.

The General's face was stern. "This person who insulted your sister. You challenged him, of course, gave him the choice of weapons. I was asking, did he die on the spot or did he linger?"

Colin's face got flaming red. His neck was hot, too. "Well, I—" he began.

The General's eyes were blazing. "You mean he was a bounder. He refused the challenge and has since been dropped from all of his clubs?"

Kathy was puzzled. "He was George Swenson," she said, "and he is Colin's best friend. He plays at our house all of the time and he—"

"Skip it," Colin shouted at her. "Pipe down and shut up!"

"Your brother is right," the General told her, his face

flushed. "The name of this cad must never again be mentioned in good society."

Then the Countess suddenly leaned forward across the teatable and smiled at Kathy. "I collect china and I would adore to see your teacup."

At this Colin felt again that funny, funny thing he had felt the last time he was here—a frightening thing, a cold thing as though a cold breeze had blown into the room.

"Teacup?" Kathy had a little cake halfway to her mouth. "What teacup?"

Colin was cross. "I told you to bring it. That teeny, teeny teacup." Then the same thing happened. He saw the Countess's eyes get small and pin-pointy and the General's hand go to his sword. Kathy noticed none of these things.

"Oh, *that* teacup." Kathy remembered. She put her hand to her cheek. "I forgot it."

The Countess's voice was very low now and serious. "You—what?" she asked. "You did what?"

"I forgot it." Kathy was getting excited. "Oh no, I didn't. Now I remember, I remember."

"Of course," the Countess said. "I felt there was more to it. Do go on."

"I gave it to Sharon. She has it in her dollhouse."

The Countess and the General spoke at the same time.

"Sharon—Sharon, and who is Sharon?"

Colin and Kathy and Loretta were all about to shout, "baby sister" when the General raised his forefinger.

"One moment, I believe I have it in here." He leafed quickly through the notebook. Then he looked pleased. "Here it is. I'll read what I have. 'Sharon Louise Mason, 805 Gaylord Street, age five and a half. Occupation, nursery school girl. Characteristics: hair, long, silky; eyes, bright; disposition, unpredictable; hobbies, dolls, paint books and thumping on piano keys with soup spoon. Unmarried.' " The General closed his notebook. "Interesting personality, that one—should go far."

The Countess agreed. "The hobby of thumping on the piano keys with a soup spoon shows great originality. It could start—a trend."

Kathy and Colin smiled. Loretta grinned. They liked to hear people speak like this about Sharon. She was the baby, the youngest, and she had always interested them, too.

Loretta said, "Sharon can play the piano with a soup spoon better than Mrs. Potts, and Mrs. Potts took lessons."

Just as quickly the Countess stopped smiling because Kathy said, "That's Sharon and she's got that teacup. Is it yours, Countess?"

Now Kathy should never have asked this question. Because now the icy thing in the room got bigger and bigger and colder and colder.

"Mine?" The Countess was playing with the rose at her waist, but her voice was as sharp as the General's sword. "Now what on earth makes you ask that?"

Then she looked at Kathy and now Kathy could see the sharp blue pin points in her eyes. She felt afraid. Colin was watching the General's hand. It was on the hilt of his sword. Suddenly Kathy laughed.

"Not yours," she cried, "I mean, maybe your little girl's in her dollhouse."

The Countess slowly sat back in her chair. The General's hand left his sword. The icy thing seemed to go out of the room.

"I have no little girl." The Countess sighed, then smiled at Kathy. "Except you and Loretta."

Loretta moaned. "My foot! Oh, my sore foot! I want to go home."

As they were leaving, the Countess took out her date book. "Tuesday at five, shall we say? Do come, and this time do bring Sharon and ask her if she would mind showing me her teacup. It's a caprice of mine."

"A—what?" asked Colin.

"A caprice," the Countess answered. "That means something you want to do for no reason except that you want to do it. So do bring Sharon."

Kathy said, "If we bring Sharon, we'll have to bring

Jerry. They play together all of the time. He's our little brother and he likes guns."

"Capital," the General told the Countess, "I like his type." And here the General snapped his fingers. "I don't give *that* for a fellow who doesn't have a drop of sporting blood in him."

They walked down the broad steps while Loretta limped behind. Colin walked with the General.

"Gee," said Colin, "the Countess has parties all the time."

"Yes," the General said, "we are quite gay here. And this is, as you know, of course, the height of the season."

"Oh, sure," Colin answered, "sure thing."

The next to the last thing the Countess said was, "I can't wait to meet Sharon and Jerry. Tell them not to dress on Tuesday. There will be—just us."

Kathy was puzzled. "Not to dress? You mean, wear night clothes?"

"Something simple," the Countess said and blew a kiss after them.

Then the very last thing she said was, "And do ask Sharon to bring the teacup."

The minute they disappeared, she walked quickly to the General's side. "Well," she asked him, "what do you think? Do they know anything? If so, how much?"

The General did not answer at once. "Frankly," he

told her, "I am puzzled. They either know nothing at all or else they know a great deal they are not telling. I don't believe for one minute that Loretta broke her foot."

"Nor I," said the Countess. "But that was not the most suspicious thing of all. The most suspicious thing of all was when Loretta said, 'Let's go home.' Always before this she has said—'go back.' "

The General sighed. "I noticed that, my dear. I hoped you had not."

She did not answer for a moment, then exclaimed, "They are all far more clever than they would have us believe. I will not feel safe until I have that teacup back in my china closet again!"

He gave her his hand and they started up the steps.

10. AN ERMINE JACKET

Tonight Mother was going out to a party with friends. She would wear, she decided, her short yellow satin and her white ermine jacket. And since she had a busy day before her, she would lay both of them out now on her bed with her slippers and evening bag. She found the yellow satin dress, but she could not find her ermine jacket.

At first she said, "It's here! It's got to be here." But it did not "got to be there," because it was not there. Three times she took everything out of her closet; her red and black dress, her brown dress with the pink dots which Colin called her "broken-out" dress.

Everything was there except the ermine jacket. She

dialed the fur man. Perhaps she was mistaken and they had not returned it. But the man said, "You came and got it yourself, three weeks ago, ma'am. You signed the slip. I kept the slip."

Mother went back upstairs to go through the closet again.

Now if she had looked out the back window and up the alleyway Mother would have seen her white ermine jacket and her white satin party slippers and her pearl earrings on their way to school.

Kathy felt very grand in the white ermine jacket. She ran her hands happily over the soft white ermine. There were deep pockets too, lined with satin; deep enough to hold her lunch; peanut butter sandwiches and four blue plums. The coat hung down below the hem of her skirt and the sleeves came far down below her hands but she kept pushing them back up. She wished the Countess could see her now!

But at every few steps, one of the heels of the white satin slippers would buckle under her and she would fall. By the time she came to the Swenson back yard, she had lost one of the pearl earrings and her lipstick was smeared from one of the falls. But the rouge was still bright, like poppies on her cheeks, and her eyebrows were smooth and black. They came all the way across her forehead without stopping, like one train track. The mascara on her eyelashes had blurred a bit and some of it was now running onto the rouge.

Kathy was so busy trying to keep afoot on the spike heels that she did not see George Swenson and Whitey Boggs standing by the Swenson garage beside their bikes. But they saw her. It was easier for them. There were two of them.

Whitey Boggs poked his sharp bony elbow into George Swenson's stomach. "Look at that." He was interested but he was calm.

But George Swenson was not calm at the sight of Kathy stumbling up the alley in her mother's coat and shoes. Maybe this was because he came from a family of one boy and five sisters. He scowled. Whenever he saw people dressed in clothes belonging to their mothers, it always seemed to George as though they were trying to make him look foolish.

"She don't come by here," he muttered under his breath. And he wheeled his bicycle out into the alley and stood there holding it like a fence.

When Kathy did see them she wished they were not there. She said nothing. She tried to push the bike out of the way. George was holding it fast and firm.

"Take your hands off my bike," he said.

She pushed again, and then she had to bend over to get one ermine cuff out of the pedal of his bike.

GAS

"I said," George glowered, "keep your hands offa my bike."

Kathy was anxious to get to school and show her white coat to the girls in her class.

"Take your bike out of my way, George Swenson. You'll make me late to school." Then she remembered something. "You should be dropped from all of your clubs and your name never mentioned again. That's what people say about you."

George did not know what she was talking about, but this only made him more cross. "Some nerve," he said, and held tighter to his bike. "That coat don't fit you and neither do them shoes. You look goofy."

Kathy was breathing hard and pushing at the bicycle. "Goofy," she was saying. "Oh you—you—cad!"

Now there is a type of older person who always tells people, "Me, I'm not the type that quarrels. I just walk away." Kathy believed in this, too. She believed in walking away from a quarrel—and finding a rock.

So she took off the jacket and shoes and rolled them all together and put them under a bush on the back lawn of the house next door to the Swenson's. Then she found a rock.

"Look out, George," his friend called, "she's got a rock."

At the sight of her face and her burning eyes, George

Swenson jumped on his bike and began to pedal quickly up the alley with Kathy running after him.

That night they were all having dinner when there was a ring at the doorbell. Rosalie came into the living room.

"It's Mrs. Newby, up the street," Rosalie told Mother. "She says she found your white ermine jacket under a bush in her back yard."

Mother jumped up from the table. "My best jacket?" Her voice was unbelieving. "My very best white ermine jacket under a bush in somebody's yard?"

"She said," Rosalie went on, "that she saw a little girl leave it there this morning."

"Please ask her to come in." Mother's voice was choked. "And Loretta, will you please come here to me?"

Kathy had stopped eating her mashed potatoes. She sat very still. But Mother was looking at Loretta.

Colin, Jerry and Sharon watched Loretta push back her chair and walk slowly over to Mother. Loretta was used to being called in that tone, in school and out at the Potts farm. So she knew how to do the "Come here to me" walk. She walked slowly, her hands in her pocket, chin held down.

She hadn't been listening when Rosalie came into the room and told about Mrs. Newby and the coat. So she didn't yet know what she had done.

"Why did you do it, Loretta?"

Loretta kept silent. Do what? she wondered. What have I done now? If she waited she would find out.

Mother was explaining. "I want to know why, Loretta. I want to know why you took my white ermine coat and put it under a bush."

Every eye in the room was on her. That is every eye but Kathy's. Kathy was looking at the china closet, wondering how soon she could run out of the room. But there stood Rosalie at the door to the kitchen and Mother at the door to the hall.

"Loretta!" Mother took her by the shoulders and shook her. "What am I going to do with you? Oh, what am I going to do?"

Now Mother was not asking for reasons, she was asking for advice. Loretta gave her some.

"I'll tell you what you can do," she said. "You can stop shaking me and give me some more potatoes. I'm hungry."

Mother leaned against the wall. "Upstairs!" She pointed to the stairs. "You and I are going upstairs. Right now."

She took Loretta by the arm and was about to take her upstairs when Mrs. Newby stepped into the room with a paper parcel under her arm.

"I left a roast in the oven," she said, "to return your coat to you."

Mrs. Newby was a rather sweet-looking little woman who dressed in funny clothes and talked to the birds. In fact people said of her that she was "with the birds." But there were none of them with her tonight as she stepped into the dining room. She had a gray shawl wrapped around her shoulders and there was a large old-fashioned type of watch pinned to her blouse. It was the type of watch people used to call a "turnip." She mentioned this.

"Excuse this old turnip." She pointed to it. "But it is the only thing in my house which tells me anything. Mr. Newby tells me nothing."

Kathy slid under the table and lay there hiding.

Mother took the bundle which Mrs. Newby handed her.

"Thank you so much for your trouble, Mrs. Newby. I am about to have a few words with this young lady." And Mother held fast to Loretta's arm.

"A few words," said Mrs. Newby. "The fewer the better. It's actions that count in this world. My, it's good to sit down."

And she sat down at the dining room table and kicked off her shoes.

"Now why are you hanging onto that girl there? Can't

she stand up by herself? Sit down here with me. Yes, thank you, I will have some dessert with you."

So there was nothing for Mother to do but dish her up some pudding and sit down with her while she ate it.

"If I am not too forward," she said, spooning the pudding, "why were you dragging that child upstairs for a few words in the middle of a meal?"

Mother's voice was firm. "She must learn a lesson. She must learn to leave other people's things alone, and when she doesn't she must tell the truth about it."

Mrs. Newby took another mouthful of pudding. "A fine thing to learn—that. I should have learned that years ago. Well, I'll be going."

She went toward the door.

"Your shoes, Mrs. Newby." Mother reminded her.

"I'm always forgetting them," Mrs. Newby smiled. "But I usually leave them on the bus. This is nothing like a bus. I must be dreamy today. Oh, I have my dreamy days and my sharp days. I was wondering just which this was. Now I know and I thank you for it."

She leaned down to get her shoes and as she did her eyes looked square into Kathy's under the table. She straightened up.

"It's all right, of course, to keep children under the table. In my day they didn't do it, but then times are changing." Again she walked to the door.

She pointed toward the table. "The coat was too big

for her," she said, "much too big for her." And she opened the door and was halfway out before Mother realized what she had said.

"Mrs. Newby, just a minute." Mother asked, "What was that you said?"

Mrs. Newby was rather an odd character.

"I do not chew my cabbage twice," she answered, "and never did. Good night."

But Mother ran to the door. "Mrs. Newby," she begged, "wait one minute, please."

"Oh well, if you say please, then I'm helpless." And Mrs. Newby stepped back into the room. "That's a word I can't resist."

Mother dragged Kathy out from under the table. "Mrs. Newby, is this the girl who put my ermine coat under your bush?"

Mrs. Newby shook her head back and forth. "It's not really a bush, even though we sometimes call it a bush. It's really a small tree. So if you will change that question and ask me, is this the girl who put the ermine coat under a small tree? Then I will answer."

Mother patiently asked it again, as Kathy, her eyes blazing, wriggled and squirmed like a wildcat and tried to get away.

"Is this the girl who put my ermine coat under your small tree?"

Mrs. Newby nodded her head. "That's the girl. I

watched her do it and I wondered why she was doing it. If she wanted to make me a present of the coat, why didn't she bring it up to the door? Good night." She went out.

"A dreary creature," Colin said.

Mother was so surprised she stopped. Her arm that was about to shake Kathy hung in mid air. But there he was sitting quite calmly whittling with his knife on a stick.

Mother sighed and shook Kathy.

"Kathy, why did you take my ermine coat?"

"Because it was white," she said, "and white is so me."

"What," Mother gasped—"what did you say?"

"Oh, Mother," Kathy's voice was patient. "She saw it right away."

"She?" Mother looked so puzzled. "And who—who is she?"

Kathy put an elegant hand to her hair.

"Don't be dull, Mother. When you are dull, you bore me."

"Answer me." Mother was shaking her harder now. "Who is—she?"

"She," began Kathy, beginning to cry. "She—"

"Kathy," cried Colin, jumping up from his chair. "Kathy—shhh!"

And so Kathy stood there, saying nothing.

Finally Mother went over to Loretta. "Loretta, dear, why didn't you tell me you hadn't taken my coat?"

"I don't know," Loretta answered, and she didn't. But she had something else to say. She pointed at Kathy. "Does she get to have an ermine coat and Irene Irene Lavene, too?"

"Go to bed, all of you!" cried Mother as she picked up her beautiful white ermine coat, now ripped and stained with plum juice and peanut butter.

She wept over the coat for a few minutes, and then she lifted her head and began to worry.

What had come over Kathy? She had never done anything like this before—ever. And yes, there was that sly, secret look in her eyes when she said, "she," that Colin had in his eyes the day the policemen had found him in the Jaguar. Was it catching like the measles? Had Loretta brought it home with her?

And who was "she?"

Mother decided then and there that she would find out who "she" was. She would watch them carefully. She would follow them!

11. A WONDERFUL BASEMENT

If Colin had known that this was the last time he would ever go to a party in the castle across the bridge, he might have looked at everything more carefully, the way one does when doing anything for the last time.

But he was uneasy today for two reasons. First, it had not been easy to slip away from Mother. She had been watching him so carefully!

Every time he left the house even to go to school or the store she followed him; driving slowly in her car or walking half a block behind and stepping quickly behind a bush or into a doorway when he turned to look back.

She had been acting like a "private eye" in a detective story on TV.

This afternoon, for instance, he had had to pretend he was going up the street to play with George Swenson. He'd watched her slip out the back way and get into her car before he could get the others and run quickly upstairs into Loretta's clothes closet.

He was uneasy in the second place today as he watched Kathy run ahead of them over the bridge because he had Sharon by one hand and Jerry by the other. He was never supposed to take "the little ones" away from the house without permission. He could tell they were frightened at the middle of the bridge by the way they were pinching his fingers. Suddenly he felt much taller, and there was a moment when he thought of his mother sitting in her car in the driveway and he felt sorry and ashamed.

This was the first visit they had ever made without Loretta.

But Loretta was not interested any more in the castle over the bridge.

She was interested in getting to school on time and helping with the dishes. The teacher often found her sitting on the steps when she came to open the schoolhouse at eight in the morning.

And Rosalie had to keep telling her, "You're only supposed to dry the dishes, not polish them till the flowers come off."

And she didn't say "Ma'am" any more. She said "Mother."

"Mother, I'm staying, Mother, after school, Mother, to help, Mother, the teacher, Mother, clean the erasers, Mother."

Now as Colin approached the bridge he whispered to the little ones, "Don't get scared. It's fun——you'll see."

But at the dizziest part of the bridge, Sharon let go of him and put her hands across her stomach. "Ouch," she cried out and doubled up. "Ouch!"

He pulled her to her feet. "Keep moving," he said, "and keep hold of my hand."

It was a warm Indian summer afternoon. The weather was so nice that Sharon and Kathy and Colin had not worn jackets to school. Sharon was in a little red cotton dress with a wide sash and Jerry wore his Levis, a T-shirt and his leather belt with guns.

But when they crossed over the bridge, Colin stopped suddenly in surprise. The Countess and the General were not on the steps.

"Look," cried Kathy, "someone's waving—down there."

And sure enough, Olaf, the butler, was standing by a big door in the stone wall underneath the stone stairs.

He signaled to them to come there. Puzzled, they walked slowly to the big door. The butler opened it, bowed and said, "Ladies and gentlemen. Please step inside."

They stepped in, stopped and gasped. It was snowing! Snow was coming down thick and fast and soft, like a white blanket. They stared so hard they forgot to shiver in their light clothes. Then they heard someone laughing. They looked.

In the middle of the snowstorm stood a beautiful woman in a long black fur coat, fur mittens and fur boots; a small fur hat on her blond head. She threw back her head and laughed, then looked at them and smiled. And as always, her smile said, "How wonderful you are! How long I have waited for you!"

Jerry did not know his mouth was open until he tasted snow on his tongue. He swallowed the snow and said, "Gosh!"

Then he heard a delicious sound. He heard a horse neigh. It was a whinnying neigh, neigh sound. Sharon tried to make a sound like that.

"Neigh-ay-ay-ay," she said.

"Shh—" Colin poked her. "Look there."

And behind the smiling Countess, they could now see through the thick snowflakes, the dim outline of a big shiny black sleigh with brass bells and four black horses, stamping their feet, tossing their manes. There was a man sitting in the sleigh, holding the reins. He wore a fur coat and fur hat like those of the Countess. He took a whip out of the socket and waved it on high.

"Cheerio," he cried out. " Welcome everybody."

The Countess was bending down now and looking into Sharon's face. Colin was so excited he forgot to introduce his brother and sister.

"Gosh," he cried out. "Snow—where'd you get it? A sleigh! Horses!"

Jerry was jumping up and down. "Look at the horses! Look at the horses!"

"I love your hat," Kathy told the Countess, "and your fur coat, too."

The Countess lifted Sharon's hand and shook it. "I am delighted to see you, my dear. It was so kind of you to come. I know you are so busy."

"What?" said Sharon, and she pulled her hand away and got very close to Colin. Colin patted her.

"She's—well—she's young," he said, "not six till next summer."

"She is adorable," said the Countess, and then she held out her hand to Jerry. "I have heard so much about you, I feel I know you very well."

Jerry smiled and his dimples showed. Then he turned his head away shyly. The Countess liked this. "Reserved," she told Colin. "So becoming in a young man.

I adore reserve." Then she clapped her hands.

"And now," she cried out, "shall we go for a sleigh ride before we have tea?"

"Oh boy," said Colin, "that sounds sharp."

So the Countess picked Jerry up in her arms and carried him over to the sleigh and put him into the back seat. Then she did the same with Sharon. Kathy jumped in by herself.

"Sit next to me," she begged the Countess.

"Dear child," said the Countess, "I shall. I shall."

Colin got in the front seat with the General. First he got in beside him, but the General stood up, stepped outside and handed him the reins.

"Take the reins, old man."

"Who—me?" Colin couldn't believe his ears.

"Keep a firm hold." The General ran around and got in on the other side. "High-spirited, these beasts."

And as the Countess covered the children in the back seat with a warm fur robe, tucking them in as carefully as though they were in bed, Colin held the reins and waited for the signal.

The Countess lifted her gloved hand. "All ready," she cried. "Let's go."

There was a sudden heave forward as the four black horses leapt into the air. It was so sudden, Colin was almost jolted out of his seat. But he hung on. And the sleigh was sliding along and the brass bells on the horses went, "jingle, jingle." Colin was sitting on the edge of the seat, holding onto the reins for dear life and things began to whiz by.

Later he tried to remember what it was that whizzed by. From the corner of his eye he thought he caught a glimpse of lights burning away back in a forest, of mountaintops rising in the distance through the thick curtain of snow. But maybe he didn't. He was never sure.

But it was all cold and snow, and whatever road they were traveling seemed to stretch out far and mysterious, and the day seemed to be getting lower and darker and all the delicious feelings and sounds of a late winter afternoon were wrapped around them with the blanket of snow. He could hear the Countess laughing in the back seat. Next to him sat the General, his head buried in his fur collar, his cheeks red.

Colin had a fur robe over his knees, but his arms were getting cold. It was a long time before he noticed this. He only noticed it because his arms began to ache from holding those black leathery reins in his fingers. Then he realized his hands were cold, too.

Colin heard Kathy and Sharon in the back seat.

Sharon cried out, "Don't pull the blanket away, I'm cold."

"Me, too," said Jerry.

He heard the Countess say, "One has to feel cold before one can feel warm. Feel cold a little longer."

The wind began to blow and now it blew the snow into Colin's eyes and his mouth and all over his hair. And the water fell down the neck of his shirt as the snow hit his body. He could hardly get his breath. He could hardly see the black, straining bodies of the horses.

Colin wanted to cry out, "Stop! Stop! Let me get my breath." But he didn't. He hung on because he knew that if you hang on long enough, there comes a moment when everything changes. So he gritted his teeth and the water from his eyes fell on his cheeks. The General leaned over and said something to him. But the wind was roaring and he couldn't hear him.

Colin started to ask, "What? What did you say, sir?" But the wind blew into his mouth and he was gasping and choking.

Then he wasn't choking so much. Were the horses going slower? Yes. He was sure of it now. He could see their black backs more clearly as the wind seemed to shift. Then they stopped.

The Countess cried, "Time for tea, by the fire." Gosh that sounded good!

The General leaned over, took the reins, fastened them and jumped out. Colin's arms were stiff and cold as he leaned back into the seat of the sleigh. The leather was wet with melted snow. It felt slippery under his fingers.

Colin turned his head to see his brother and sisters. The Countess and the General were helping them down out of the big sleigh.

"And now," the Countess clapped her hands, "come over and let us turn off the snow."

Colin forgot that he was cold. Through the winter they walked only a few steps, and then he saw a wall. There was a red button on it which said "Snow" in white letters. The Countess smiled at him. "Press it, Colin."

He pressed it. There was a whirring sound, like machinery running down, going a—erp—ah—erp—slurp—stop! As though a thousand white curtains had been pulled by wires up to a ceiling. And now it was possible to see where you were.

They were standing in a corner of a great, vast room, bigger than the gym at school. There were the sleigh and the horses standing in the center of the room, with puddles of water all around from the melting snow.

They had been driving round and round this big room and yet it had seemed like forever in a great big place. It was the Countess's basement.

"Gosh," thought Colin, "they are even richer than I'd thought; even have their own snow!"

Now they were in the library. The General helped

himself to a hamburger and brought one to Colin.

"Great outing! Makes a man's blood race, eh?"

"Yes," said Colin.

It was not until they had each had six hamburgers and hot dogs that the Countess mentioned the teacup. She spoke to Sharon.

"My dear," she smiled, "I would adore to see your teacup."

Sharon stared at her. She did not know what she was talking about.

Kathy jumped up off the floor. "I brought it," she said, putting her hand into her pocket. "I almost forgot it, then I remembered. I got it out of Sharon's doll-house."

"You give it to me," Sharon cried out. "It's mine. You gave it to me."

"Why, just look." Kathy was so surprised as she reached into her pocket and drew out, not a tiny teacup, but a full-sized teacup.

"How did this get here? This isn't Sharon's little tea-cup. This is a big cup."

She was holding it in her hand wonderingly, when the Countess reached out and grabbed it so quickly, Kathy was startled. The Countess laughed softly. "My dear, I beg your pardon. I'm sorry I frightened you." But she held the teacup tightly in her hand. Her eyes seemed to say, "At last, at last." She walked to the table and set it alongside the other cups. "How odd," she said, "it seems to match my set."

Then she turned those eyes, so cold now and so pin-pointy, upon Kathy. Kathy shivered, she didn't know why.

"Where did you get it?"

Kathy answered slowly, "I don't know. I don't know where I got it. I—I didn't know I had it. It was a teeny, teeny, teeny one I put into my pocket."

"Yes," nodded the Countess, "and what happened to the teeny, teeny, teeny one, as you call it?"

"I don't know." Kathy was puzzled. "I guess it fell out of my pocket."

"Of course." The Countess smiled as though she were pleased. "But tell me and I hope I don't bore you—"

"Oh, no," Kathy murmured, "that's all right."

"I can understand that the teeny cup fell out of your pocket and you don't know how you got this big cup, but wherever did you get the teeny cup in the first place?"

Kathy thought. "Let me think," she began.

Then Colin remembered. He suddenly remembered that Rosalie had said she found that cup in his bathrobe. Had Rosalie told Kathy about this? His eyes went to the General. Yes, his hand was still on his sword and he was standing very close to Kathy. Sharon and Jerry sat very still. They did not understand what was happening, but they knew that feeling which always said, "Something's happening! Something's wrong! Sit up straight! Keep very still! Listen! Wait!"

The pin points in the Countess's eyes had never seemed so pin-pointy. Colin stopped breathing. There was not a sound in the room except the fire crackling in the fireplace. Finally Kathy spoke. "Well," she said, "it was in the morning. I remember that. I was brushing my teeth and somebody—somebody said, 'Here's something for your dollhouse.' "

"Yes," urged the Countess, "go on."

"Sharon wanted it." Kathy smiled now and shrugged. "And I gave it to her. That's all."

"Not quite," said the General. "Not quite, Madame."

"You," the Countess waved at him to hush, "you were a sweet child to give the cup to your sister. But who—who was the somebody who gave it to you?"

Kathy thought again. "I can't remember," she answered.

"Very convenient, Madame," growled the General.

But Kathy was saying, "It wasn't Sharon, because I gave it to her. It wasn't Colin or Jerry—" and here Colin felt the breath go out of him in a sigh of relief. "They're boys, and boys don't play with teacups, only girls."

The Countess and the General exchanged a long look.

The General said slowly, "Could it, could it—have been—Loretta?"

"Loretta!" Kathy's voice was so surprised. "I never thought of Loretta."

And as the Countess and General exchanged a look, the look seemed to say, "But *we* had!"

"She is a girl," the General reminded her. "Only girls play with teacups."

"Maybe it was Loretta," Kathy agreed, "but I can't remember."

They waved good-bye to the children as they went down the stone steps, across the bridge and disappeared into the forest.

Then the General's face grew hard.

"Didn't I tell you?" he reminded the Countess. "In the words of the underworld—Loretta is our pigeon."

"I still cannot believe it." And the Countess was so unhappy. "I have loved Loretta for so long and she has loved me. Why would she disobey me? Why would she take something from my house after all of these years?"

"I warned you, my dear." The General's face was stern. "I warned you days ago. This is serious, and remember your weakness."

She sighed. "I know, I know." And she put her hand on his arm.

"And someday," he reminded her, "it will destroy all of us."

The Countess's face grew more serious. "You are right. We cannot take the chance. Loretta must be punished. But how? She has stopped coming here lately. She may never come back again." And here the Countess's face turned white and she grabbed his arm. "General, is it possible she has discovered the secret of the bridge and she may tell it to them? How—oh how—can we find out? How can we get her here to find out?"

The General twirled his mustache and smiled a wintry smile.

"My dear, you have always underestimated me. I began steps in that direction days ago. You recall the dreary couple at the foot of our hill?"

"Mr. and Mrs. Potts?" And here the Countess was so surprised. "How can those unattractive people ever entice Loretta back to our hill—to us?"

He turned gracefully and lifted her hand to his lips.

"I took care to destroy their crops in one night. And I took care to dry up their milk cows in the twinkling of an eye. I believe, my dear Countess, that we can trust their greedy little hearts to do the rest."

"Of course," and the Countess clapped her white hands.

"Oh, I am so proud of you, General."

And he was very proud of himself.

12. IRENE IS GONE

And the General could well be proud of himself. Because even as the children were having tea in the Countess's library, Mr. and Mrs. Potts were parking their old Chevrolet at the curbing before Mother's house.

Mother was fitting a sweater on Loretta. She had been knitting it for her for weeks. It had white reindeer running across the chest and Loretta was standing still as Mother fitted it on. Never in her life had she stood so still.

Mother did not need to take long with the fitting. But she had to keep busy, she told herself; busy so she would not think.

"Are you sure, Loretta," she asked her again, "that you do not know where the children went?"

And Loretta always answered in a foolish way, Mother thought. She either said things like, "Whose children?" or else she said, "What makes you think I know where they went?"

Then Mother saw Mr. and Mrs. Potts standing on the front porch with a package.

"Run upstairs, Loretta, and I will deal with them."

Loretta ran upstairs but she hid at the top to listen.

When Mr. Potts sat down he wiped at his eyes with a blue bandana handkerchief. "You never know you'll miss a young 'un till she's gone."

Mother was so astonished. "You miss Loretta?"

"I baked her this cake," said Mrs. Potts, and she handed Mother a chocolate cake wrapped in a newspaper. On the cake in white candy letters it said, "Loretta–gone but not forgotten."

Mother was touched.

"Oh, thank you, Mrs. Potts. This is so kind of both of you."

Mr. Potts spoke now.

"We didn't miss her at first as much as we've missed her the last week," he said. "The crops has all failed. The cows won't give milk. And that showed us how much we miss her."

Then he leaned forward. "That hill misses her, too," he said. "At night on the wind we hear voices calling—'Loretta—Loretta.' "

Mrs. Potts hitched her chair forward. "Send the gal back to us, ma'am. She didn't want to leave us in the first place—remember?"

Mother was shocked. "Send her back to you! I wouldn't think of it," she said. "She's getting along fine. Her schoolwork is better. She minds me." Here Mother's face grew sad.

"It's the others who have changed," she told them. "They go away some place and when they return they look sly and secret. They speak in a strange manner and they pull away when I put my arms around them. Yes, Loretta is fine, but since she came home nothing has been the same."

Mr. Potts pulled at his mustache.

"All the more reason you should send her back to us," he said, "and let things be like they was for everybody before you took her back."

Mother started to say, "No, no," again but just then she heard a noise. "Excuse me, one moment," and she hurried upstairs.

There they all were, Colin and Kathy and Jerry and Sharon. Their clothes were damp as though they had been in a storm. And on the faces of each was that sly, secret smile!

"Sharon! Jerry!" Mother ran to them first. "Where have you been? How did your clothes get so damp?"

And Sharon pulled away from her. "Don't maul me," she said. "You bore me."

Jerry turned his head from her. "I don't like it here. I want to go back there—with Them."

Sharon pouted. "Why can't we have snow in our basement?"

Colin and Kathy grabbed them and cried out, "Shh-shh, you promised!"

"Go to your rooms," said Mother finally.

Then she sat down on the top step of the stairs and thought and thought.

Nothing *had* been the same since Loretta came home. Colin and Kathy had changed first, and now the little ones. The babies, too, had that sly secret smile, just like the smile Loretta had had the first day she got lost in the woods behind the Potts farm. Was it catching, like the measles? Yes, Mother decided. She used to have four good children and one naughty girl. Now she had one good girl and four naughty children.

She jumped up. Yes, she had to do it. It would break her heart but it was better to have four good children again than keep Loretta here at home. Besides, hadn't the Pottses admitted they had missed Loretta? And Loretta had never wanted to come home in the first place.

"Rosalie," Mother called, "pack Loretta's things,

please. She is going back to live with Mr. and Mrs. Potts, and she is going back now."

Loretta's room was empty as Rosalie went over to the closet and took out the old brown-paper suitcase, opened the drawers of the dresser, took out the nice new underwear and nightgowns and laid them carefully in the case. She took down the hangers of little cotton dresses and the little blue serge suit and threw them across the bed.

Kathy came in and asked right away, "What are you doing, Rosalie?"

"I'm packing a suitcase for Loretta. She's going away—back to the Potts farm."

Kathy ran out of the room, and in a minute she came back followed by Colin and Jerry and Sharon. Silently they watched Rosalie pack.

"Loretta going away? Why?"

Rosalie straightened up. "You're the reason why. Your mother thinks it's her fault cops came to the house, ermine coats got found under bushes, bad grades in school, funny highfalutin talk and damp clothes."

The children disappeared into their own rooms like four wooden cuckoo birds into four wooden clocks. Each one felt uneasy.

Colin thought, "Loretta didn't make me get into that red Jaguar."

Kathy thought, "Loretta didn't make me take that ermine coat."

Jerry and Sharon thought, "Loretta didn't turn on the snow."

All this time Loretta was hiding in the upstairs broom closet. She had heard everything Mother and Rosalie had said. Now when she heard the suitcase thumping against the steps of the stairs as Rosalie carried it down, she ran quickly down the hall. She waited outside Kathy's room until she saw Kathy hurry downstairs.

Just as she thought. Kathy had left the door open.

Loretta had not seen Irene Irene Lavene for weeks now. And even though she knew she must hurry, she had to stand one minute and admire her. She was so beautiful! There she sat, her arms outstretched, her little dancer's skirt stiff and saucy, her little red satin shoes shiny and silky, her soft little arms and knees, so dimpled and sweet.

Instead of picking her up this time, Loretta lifted up the chair, hurried down the hall, ran into her own room and into the closet.

Rosalie thought she heard Irene Irene Lavene singing and then decided Kathy was playing with her. It only sounded for a minute—just long enough to hear her sweet voice raised in "Don't leave me, dearest playmate or I will surely die," and then all was quiet—nothing.

Mr. Potts was standing in the living room holding Loretta's suitcase as Rosalie went all through the house and out into the yard calling her.

"Loretta," she called, "Loretta Mason Potts—you come in here."

Whitey Boggs heard her as he rode by the house on his bike.

"Loretta—Loretta Mason Potts, you come in here," he mocked.

When they told Mother that Loretta was gone, she did a strange thing. She cried. "My poor child! What has happened to her?

Mr. Potts took it lightly. "She'll come back; a bad penny always comes back. And when she does you call me, and me and Ma'll come in and fetch her."

Colin said nothing. He knew where Loretta had gone. And then Kathy ran out of her room shrieking, "Irene is gone; Irene Irene Lavene is gone!"

Mother stopped crying. "She really is a naughty girl. Oh, what a naughty girl!"

Kathy suddenly stopped crying. She whispered to Colin. "I know where she's gone, don't you?"

He nodded.

"And she took Irene Irene over there. I will go over there and get Irene back."

Irene Is Gone

"I'll go with you," Colin promised. "Tonight after supper."

13. A KIDNAPPING

The Countess was smiling as she stepped through the gold and white doors of her ballroom into her drawing room.

It was a beautiful party. Now she would order the supper. She was halfway across the room before she saw the awful thing. It was part of a monster! It was a great leg and foot thrust through her front door! It was lying across the rug in the hallway!

The leg was pink and the shoe on the foot was red, red satin with red satin straps tied across the great ankle. The tip of the red satin shoe was on a level with a small table in the hallway where the Countess kept a silver salver for calling cards.

A Kidnapping

The Countess was so horrified, so angry, that for a moment she could not speak.

"How dare they? How could they? How could any large creature get over the bridge?"

Then she screamed, "Get out! Get out of my house!"

Servants came running into the hall from the kitchen, a cook in a white cap, and three waiters. They looked and ran back in terror.

"Cowards, cowards!" She stamped her foot. "Come back here. Throw it out. Close my door. Call the General."

He ran into the room. He unsheathed his sword. "Stand back," he called, "everybody stand back. I will slay the beast."

He placed one hand on his hip, lunged forward, ran his sword into the great foot. He pulled out the sword and looked at the shining blade.

"No blood!" He was amazed. "You see, my dear, absolutely not one drop of blood."

"Attack again!" she cried. "Again! Again!"

Again the General lunged and attacked, this time through the calf of the leg. Again he withdrew the sword and examined it. No blood! He stepped closer to examine the wound. There was a small hole in the leg like a puncture in a tire. He bowed low.

"Countess, if I may say something?"

"Anything, anything," she kept screaming. "Say anything, do anything, get it out of here."

"This creature is not alive."

"What? What did you say?" She held up the skirts of her ball gown and came closer to it. "Not alive?" Closing her eyes and turning her head away, she put forth her hand fearfully to touch it. But first she asked, "General, you're sure it's not alive?"

"Positive," he answered. "It was for knowing such things I received these," and he flipped the medals on his chest.

She touched the big leg, lightly at first, with one finger. She looked at the finger. "You are right, General," she nodded slowly. "This leg is made of hard rubber or some similar material. It is definitely not alive."

They tiptoed to the window and looked outside. They saw a great creature in a yellow dress sitting on top of the bridge, one foot stretched across the stairs and into the door of the house, another across the stream. One arm rested on the roof and her great head with yellow hair was on a level with the chimneys.

A giant, a blond giant, on their bridge, her clumsy limb thrust rudely into the house. Her glassy eyes looked up at the night. The coarse creature was wearing a garish yellow dancing dress.

"Oh, the atrocious taste of her! Come on." The

Countess took the General's arm. "There is nothing to be learned unless we climb up on her as one climbs a mountain. Keep your sword ready, just in case."

With the General assisting her, the Countess jumped up onto Irene Irene's leg and walked up it. It was like walking up a large, round log. She almost lost her balance several times, but the General caught her.

Once, as they walked through the stiff tulle of the dancing skirt, the Countess had to reach out and grab a handful to keep from falling.

"I'm falling," she gasped.

"Me, too," said the General.

But the Countess now seized hold of the sash around Irene Irene's waist, and the General seized hold of her and the two of them teetered for a moment while the General cried out, "Hold on, my dear, hold on tight."

"I'm holding on, you idiot!" she told him. "Do something, say something—sensible!"

They looked rather odd, standing there on Irene's dancing skirt, clinging to the yellow sash around her middle.

"What if it rips?" the General gasped.

"A stupid remark," the Countess answered. "If it rips, we fall into the stream."

So for a moment they said nothing, but hung on.

The General spoke first. "The creature is definitely

not alive. No live female would endure this. We are tearing her dress. Let us climb up or climb down."

Then from the sky they heard a great voice booming through the night air. The Countess was so startled she let go of Irene's sash.

"Help me," she screamed. "I'm falling! Ooh—" And she fell into the stream with a splash!

The next splash was the General's.

The booming voice went on. The Countess staggered through the water to the bank.

"Judgment Day, General. It's the Judgment Day!"

"My sword," he wailed as he waded in the water. "I've lost my sword."

But he stood still and listened as the voice boomed on. The Countess climbed out of the stream and sat gasping on the bank, her clothes soaking wet, her hair damp, her eyes frightened.

Just as suddenly as it began, the voice stopped.

"Judgment Day!" the Countess was breathing hard and feeling her ear lobes for her diamond earrings. "It is the Judgment Day."

The General had found his sword. He was wearing his high, black leather boots. His feet were dry. He was taking the whole thing much better than the Countess.

"Judgment Day?" The water splashed as he waded toward her. "Perhaps, but the words were not highly inspiring. I had thought to hear better on Judgment Day."

"The words?" The Countess had been so frightened she had not tried to hear the words.

But the General, despite his fright had listened. "Military training, my dear," he explained. "A cool head in a crisis."

"My head is cool, too," snapped the Countess. "It is sopping wet and I have lost my diamond earrings, so don't be dull. What did the voice say?"

The General told her as he helped her to her feet. "It announced that the boy was standing on the burning deck, eating peanuts by the peck."

"Oh, no," the Countess was shocked. "Not that stupid old rhyme. 'His mother called him but he would not go because he loved his peanuts so?' "

The General nodded. "That's the one. Will you take my arm?"

The Countess pushed him away. "You mean I have been humiliated like this," she looked at her torn wet stockings, her sopping wet dress, "for a thing like that?" She stamped her foot.

"It's too much, oh it's much too much. And this," she pointed to Irene Irene, "coarse vulgar monster! Call everyone, we must get her foot out of my hallway and her arm off my roof."

A Kidnapping

The General was a brave soldier. But now he had something to do which he dreaded far more than he had ever feared a duel. He helped the Countess through the library window and guided her over to the fireplace.

"Stand there," he said. "Get warm."

For one second he stood in the door of the library. He listened to the music in the ballroom and the slush, slush, creaking sound of many feet moving in time to the music across the dance floor.

"Poor souls," he thought, "let them dance a while longer." Then he closed the door.

He looked at the Countess. He had never seen her like this before. Her dress was ruined. She stood in her stocking feet and her hair hung like a wet mop. He poured her a glass of wine, handed it to her. She lifted it to her lips. Then she saw that the General had not touched his glass. He was watching her. What she saw in his eyes made her put down the glass at once.

"General, that look on your face. You feel this trouble is that serious?"

Now he had to do it. He took her hand, "My dear, we are not in trouble."

"No?"

"No." He shook his head. "We are finished. We are undone."

"You mean?" She was puzzled.

"I mean that by now Loretta has learned our secret and has gone back to get them. The bridge was our only protection and now the bridge is occupied."

He looked around the room, at the polished wood on the walls, the beautiful rug, the tables, the books, the exquisite paintings. He waved his hand.

"One kick from one foot of one of Them—and all of this—pouf! Smashed!"

The Countess turned white.

"Oh," the General picked up his wine glass, "at first they will come out of curiosity, to see the tiny world as they would call it. And they will laugh."

"Laugh?" the Countess's voice was shocked. "Laugh at us? But how dare they?"

The General went on. "They will kneel down and peer through our windows as they would look into one of their children's dollhouses. Then one of them will reach a great hand through and seize you by the middle; and perhaps set you up on the roof while he examines you more closely."

"No, no. Oh, stop, stop!" The Countess had her hands at her ears. "General, I would never allow such a thing. Never!"

"And then," he went on, "they will put us into their pockets and take us over there. And that, my dear Countess, you would find most humiliating of all. You and I and all of our friends would be put into cages like birds. They would invite their friends to come in and stare at us.

"I can see it all now." He twirled his mustache. "Those great eyes peering in at me through the bars of a cage. Those great fingers poking me to make me move. Those great shouts of laughter."

The Countess laid a hand on his arm. "Stop, General, I can bear no more. Is there nothing we can do?"

This was the moment he was waiting for. "Yes." He stood up straight. "We can outwit them, in one way. We can all walk into the stream together and walk up a short distance where the water is over our heads."

The Countess did not speak. The General turned his head away. But she was every inch a Countess. He heard a sound. Ah, poor thing, she was weeping. No wonder! But no, she was holding up her glass and she was smiling at him.

"To you, General. It's been such fun knowing you!"

"To you, my dear, you have never looked lovelier." Then he sighed. "I would never have said it before, but now I can tell you. I have always cared deeply for you."

The Countess dropped her head. "I have suspected that."

"But you," he took her hand in his, "have only loved

children. If I had been six when we met, things might have been so different."

"Yes, General, but you were already pushing—thirty-five."

He held out his arms. "Nevertheless, before we go in and tell the others, may I have the next waltz in here?"

She stepped into his arms. "I think, General, you mean—the last waltz."

They had waltzed twice around the library, when the General heard the noise outside. He gripped the Countess's hand. "Steady, my dear, this is it."

They looked through the window.

Loretta was running up the stone staircase, taking two steps at a time. Behind her raced Sharon and Jerry. Kathy walked slowly.

"Countess, Countess, where are you?" Loretta's voice was loud and excited. "Where's the General?"

Now they could hear her frantically climbing over Irene Irene's leg, calling to the others following her, "Come on, come on, let's find the Countess."

The General opened the library door softly. "They must not see that we are frightened, remember."

Loretta ran past him. "Countess, Countess!" She was panting and out of breath. "We've been looking everywhere for you, your room, the snow room."

The Countess instantly straightened up like a knife. "You have not been back across the bridge—to tell anyone—anything?"

Loretta did not hear her. "Something terrible happened. Look out there! Irene Irene Lavene. Something happened to her. She swelled up like that just in one second. She's not a doll any more. She turned into a giant when I was bringing her across the bridge. I had to climb over her to get here."

"Me, too," said Kathy, wiping the tears from her eyes.

"So did we," said Jerry. "And me and Sharon almost fell in the stream."

"Look," Loretta cried out again, "look at her—see!"

The General was smiling a little crooked smile as he regarded the terrified children. "Who?" he asked. "What? Where?"

"See out there," Kathy sobbed. "Look—out there!"

When the Countess spoke her voice sounded so innocent.

"See—*what?* Oh, do calm down, children."

The General sauntered over to the window. He yawned. "There does seem to be something out there, Countess. Look!"

The Countess pretended at first she could not see anything.

"Where? I see nothing. What would you have me look

at General, the moon?" She smiled at the wide-eyed, frightened children. "The dear fellow is so romantic."

The General pretended to be patient. "You are looking in the wrong direction, Countess. Stand here. Now look there."

"You mean the sky, General? The trees, the big black night?"

Jerry yelled and jumped up and down. "The bridge—the bridge. Look on the bridge!"

The General leaned out of the window. He chuckled as he pulled his head back inside. "By Jove, Countess, this is a bit of a do, I must say."

Loretta took hold of the Countess's hand and pulled at her. "The doorway. Come and look at what's in your doorway!"

"Humor the child," the General urged her. "Let's have a look in the doorway."

Loretta ran ahead of them calling, "Come on—hurry. Look!"

Hand in hand, the General and the Countess sauntered after her toward the leg. But the General stopped now by a vase of flowers.

"I'll join you in a minute, my dear, but first I must have a boutonniere."

The Countess gazed calmly at the leg and the big foot with the red satin shoe. "How odd," she murmured. "I wonder, is this anyone I know?"

Loretta was getting more and more impatient. Jerry and Sharon were so surprised. Kathy still sobbed quietly.

"It's Irene!" Loretta shouted. "Irene Irene Lavene, Kathy's doll. I stole her tonight. Then she turned into a big thing as I was crossing the bridge with her."

The Countess was tapping lightly with her fingers on the red satin toe. "A doll—not really! Do come and look, General. This is rather amazing."

"One moment," he called to her and he went right on examining the vase of roses to find just the right size for his buttonhole. He made a great pretense of humming and did not turn his eyes away from the flowers.

"Let's see here," he was talking to himself. "Perhaps this natty little yellow one. Ah, yes—I will have you."

The Countess whispered to the wide-eyed children. "It takes a great deal to amaze the General. He is so widely traveled. Do forgive him."

Sharon ran to him and pulled his arm. "Look, General, can't you even look and see what's happened to Irene Irene?"

The General adjusted his monocle as he stood before the leg. Then he removed the monocle, tapped it lightly on the back of his hand. "Large woman," he announced, "and she seems to have one foot in the door." Then he laughed and slapped the leg.

Kathy moaned in anguish. Her face was stained with tears. "She's a doll—a doll. She was the most beautiful doll in the whole world and then tonight—out there—she turned from a doll and turned into a—giant."

None of the children saw that the General and the Countess were smiling at each other.

Loretta stood very still, her eyes wide with wonder. "I know," she nodded slowly, "I know what happened."

No one spoke. Everybody listened.

"It's my fault," Loretta went on slowly, "I stole her away and I got punished. You get punished when you steal things, Mother says. Poor Kathy, she was your best doll."

Then Loretta burst into loud sobs. She ran to a sofa, threw herself down on it, sobbed and kicked her feet. One of her shoes came off.

The Countess stroked her and said soothing things. "Now Loretta, dear Loretta, don't cry, Loretta."

But Kathy said, "Let her cry. It's all her fault."

Jerry said, "Wait till Mother hears."

Sharon said, "Shame on you, Loretta, shame, shame, double shame."

But all the while the Countess was smiling at the General, and he was smiling at her. They were safe. The stupid children did not realize that Irene had not changed at all. It was they who became ten inches high as they crossed over the bridge.

"I'm going home." Kathy walked slowly to the door.

"So am I," said Jerry, "but I'm going to wade across the stream. I almost fell in when I climbed over her before."

"So did I," said Sharon, "I will wade across the stream, too."

"No, no," cried the Countess quickly. They all turned.

"What I mean is, you must not wade the stream or you will all get wet."

"Never," the General echoed. "It would never do for you to get wet."

Jerry was astonished and so was Sharon. "Afraid to get wet? Who's afraid to get wet. I like to get wet. Come on, Sharon." Then he started to run.

The Countess stepped in his path. "Oh, please." She smoothed his hair, smiled at Sharon and put her arm around Kathy. "Don't go yet. I have been counting on a little chat with all of you—in the library over a dish of ice cream."

"Don't be a boor," the General slapped Jerry on the back, "and never disappoint a lady. It's not done, you know."

"Okay," said Jerry.

"What kind of ice cream?" asked Sharon.

"I don't want any," said Kathy.

"Please," begged the Countess, "for me?"

So the General held the library door. The Countess gently pulled the weeping Loretta from the sofa and took her by the hand.

"Oh, Countess," Loretta threw her arms around her, "nobody loves me but you."

"And who else," the Countess smiled, "do you need?"

The children seated themselves stiffly in the chairs in the library.

"Wait here, please." The General bowed. "While we order the refreshments." He closed the shutters at the window. "Bit of a draft."

He beckoned the Countess outside and then closed the door, locking it quickly.

"We must set fire at once to the creature on the bridge."

The Countess nodded. "A fitting end for her and anyone else who would speak that atrocious piece."

They hurried away quickly.

Jerry had heard the lock on the door click. He tried it.

"Hey," he turned to the others, "we're locked in. The General locked us in."

"Pooh," Loretta answered. "He did not. The General is nice." Then she tried the door. It was locked.

"I want to get out," cried Sharon. "I don't want to be locked in."

"Hush," said Loretta, "we can get out. I'll show you." Then she went to another door in the room, opened it and stood still in amazement. It was a closet door. And inside was a great gold watch with a black strap. On the back of the watch was engraved the name "Colin."

"Hey," Jerry pulled it out with both hands onto the carpet, "that's a watch like Colin's watch—only lots bigger."

But Loretta was looking at something else. She was holding the end of a big white tablecloth with the name "Loretta" embroidered in red thread at one corner. "My handkerchief," her tone was hushed.

"Your handkerchief!" Kathy's voice was scornful. "A big thing like that! How could that be a handkerchief?"

"It is," Loretta's voice was full of wonder. "I don't know how, but it is. I spilled ink on my handkerchief, green ink, and here it is. Look, there is the green ink."

Suddenly she understood.

"We're little," she told them, "that's what happens in the middle of the bridge. We get little. This is all—little!"

"What a pity," someone said, and then they turned slowly around. They had not heard the door open. They had not heard him come in. But there he was, the General, standing with a tray of dishes of ice cream. His eyes now were as cold as the ice cream and his lips were as straight as a ruler. He was looking beyond them to the wrist watch and the handkerchief.

"A great, great pity." Then he sighed. "The cat is out of the bag and the bloom is off the rose. Ladies and gentlemen, be seated. I suggest you find a comfortable chair, because now, you will remain here with us—forever."

Then he clicked his heels and bowed, walked through the door, closed it, locked it, taking the ice cream with him!

14. OUTWITTING THE POLICE

When Colin woke the next morning he heard sounds of feet running back and forth outside. He ran to his window.

Outside on the lawn there were groups of the neighbors, three policemen and one plain-clothes officer. They were walking on the lawn, studying the ground.

"A ladder," he heard one policeman say, "they could have used a ladder, but where're the prints?"

He ran downstairs. The dining room was empty. There were none of the breakfast time sounds and smells and hurry.

The doors of the music room opened and out stepped Mother, followed by a man in a police captain's uniform who was holding pictures of Kathy and Jerry and Sharon and Loretta.

"We'll have these pictures on all the TV newscasts within an hour," the officer was saying to her. "All the roads out of town have been blocked, and if the kidnappers act according to formula you will get a message sometime today."

Then Colin knew what had happened. He had fallen sound asleep after he went to bed, but Kathy had gone to bed and then gotten up again. She had gone through the tunnel after Irene Irene and Jerry and Sharon had gone with her.

He ran to his mother. The police captain pushed him away.

"Leave your mother alone, son. She's had a great shock."

"But, Mother!" He jerked away from the captain's hand. "Blocking roads is no good. I know where the children are."

Everybody got very still. Mother ran to him. She began to shake him. "Where are they, Colin? Tell me at once."

The words came out of Colin's mouth like popcorn popping on a hot pan. "Through the tunnel and over the bridge there's a countess and a general."

"What's that?" asked the captain, getting out his notebook. "Where?"

"It's through a tunnel and over a bridge." Colin was breathless now. "There's a big beautiful house and a general with a sword and the Countess has a snow room and a bed like a boat."

The captain sat him down in a chair. "Calm down, son. Where is this place? How do we get there? What's the address?"

"You go upstairs," Colin told him, "and you go into my sister Loretta's clothes closet and push on the wall and there's a tunnel and then a forest and then a bridge. Come on. I'll show you."

Colin was running out of the room.

But Mother and the police captain were not moving. Mother sighed.

"Please excuse him, captain. The poor boy is hysterical."

The captain put away his notebook. "He's been watching too much television or reading too many comic books."

Colin was getting more and more excited. He was shouting. "Come on," he cried, "I'll show you. The wall opens. There's a tunnel behind it."

Then he pulled at his mother. But the captain took hold of his arm. "Have you got some place you could send him, ma'am? Some place where he could stay till this is cleared up?"

Mother thought. "Yes. This is not good for him. Let him go down the street and stay with Mrs. Newby. But captain, please don't let the kidnappers get him, too."

"Now, now," the captain's voice was comforting, "we'll send two of my men with him so nobody will get him."

Then the captain called two of the other policemen from the lawn. Kicking, yelling and shouting, Colin was taken out of the house in his pajamas. Rosalie ran upstairs to get his clothes, and before you could count to five he was bundled into a police car. He saw Whitey Boggs and George Swenson in the crowd at the curbing. They were looking at him, curious and a little frightened.

As the car pulled away from the curbing he was still shouting at his mother. But she wasn't listening.

A few minutes later, Mother passed Loretta's bedroom on her way to her bathroom to get a cold towel for her head. She stopped. The wall at the back of that clothes closet. Didn't it look odd, though?

She walked over to it. It was standing like a door—ajar. Was she dreaming? She must be. She touched it. It swung open and there *was* a long black tunnel with lights. Colin had been telling the truth.

Mother did not hesitate one second, even though she was afraid. Fear? What was fear? Wherever her children had gone, she would go, no matter how terrible.

She stepped through the doorway in the wall of the closet and the door swung slowly shut behind her.

Mrs. Newby and Colin were having breakfast. That is, Mrs. Newby was sitting at her breakfast table with him. He was not eating. He was thinking of his brother and sisters.

He knew they had gone over the bridge, but why hadn't they come back? And then he knew, suddenly, why they had not come back. He remembered all of the times he had seen those pin points in the Countess's eyes and the General's hand at his sword.

His brother and sisters had not come back because they couldn't come back. They were being held. Oh, why didn't his mother listen to him? If he could only get out of here and get back home.

But there was a policeman at the back door of Mrs. Newby's house and one at the front door.

Mrs. Newby started to butter a roll for him and then she stopped. "Listen," she said, "there's a friend of mine. Hear that, outside? Hear that rat-a-tat-tat sound?"

Yes, it was a rat-a-tat-tat—pecking sound on the window pane.

"Stay here," said Mrs. Newby, "and wait for me. This may be important news."

She was back in a minute. Her face was beaming.

"Most, most interesting. This friend of mine tells me he has seen your brother and your sisters."

Colin jumped up. "Where is he? Where are they?"

"They are where you told me they were, Colin, at the house through the tunnel and across the bridge."

Colin jumped up and down. "I knew it. I knew it. I've got to go." He ran toward the door, but as he opened it the policeman stood looking down at him.

"Get back in there, bud," said the policeman, "where do you think you're going?" Colin slowly closed the door.

Then he had an idea. "Who told you, Mrs. Newby? Who told you where they were? Make him tell those cops."

Mrs. Newby smiled. "My friend is far away from here by now," she said. "And besides he wouldn't set foot in this room. You see my friend—is a robin."

Colin sat down in the chair. "A robin!" And yet he believed her. It seemed only fair. She had believed him.

"If you want to get to them," said Mrs. Newby, "you should go now and not let any grass grow under your feet."

Colin ran to the window. He pointed. "How can I get by those cops?"

Mrs. Newby thought a minute. "There is always a way. Wait right here."

She was back in a minute with a long black dress and a little checkered apron. She held the dress up for Colin to see. He drew back.

"Me, wear that?" He was horrified.

"They would let you pass," she said, "and you would even get a seat on a crowded bus. I would advise you to try it. It's been a wonderful help to me. I have dozens of them."

So, gingerly, he stepped into the black dress and Mrs. Newby fastened the apron on him and pinned it up. Then she got into her hatboxes and brought out a little black bonnet which tied under the chin. Then she found a gray shawl which she wrapped around his shoulders.

"You will find that this comes in very handy and gives you safe passage past any policemen."

Then she put little black gloves on him, and when she had finished, he looked just like a dear old lady, like a smaller version of Mrs. Newby herself. She pushed him toward the door.

"Open it and walk out. Go where you must go. Smile shyly, as though you loved the whole world and everybody in it and would never lift your hand against anyone again."

Colin started to run toward the door, but she caught him.

"Go slowly, very, very slowly."

So he started again and he had never realized how hard it would be to walk slowly when you were in a hurry. But he did it and he was about to open the door when Mrs. Newby spoke.

"Wait," she said, "the message. Now let me think, what was it? Oh yes, my friend, the robin said this: 'Don't walk over the bridge. Walk up the stream.' "

Colin was puzzled. "Up the stream? What does that mean?" But he opened the door and went out.

Mrs. Newby watched as the policemen tipped their hats to Colin and said kindly, "Good morning, Mrs. Newby."

Then she saw Colin get to the gate and start to run up the street fast, pulling the skirt up over his blue jeans. She saw the two policemen start to chase him, calling out, "Stop! Stop!" Then she couldn't see any more.

15. MOTHER IN THE TUNNEL

When Mother stepped out of the tunnel and found herself in a forest, she first thought, "I'm dreaming. I've fallen asleep and I'm dreaming."

But she remembered Colin had said the children were here. She looked around the forest and began to call them. At first her voice was low because she was puzzled and frightened. So she called softly, "Kathy, Sharon, Jerry, Loretta."

Nothing answered her. The leaves on the trees said nothing. The sun falling across the stone bridge at the end of the path was warm and yellow. Everything was silent.

She made her voice louder. She put her hands to her mouth and called louder and faster. "Kathy, Sharon, Jerry, Loretta! Come here." But no one answered.

She walked down the path to the stone bridge. They couldn't hide from her. She would find them, no matter how long it took. She stamped a foot on the stone bridge. "Kathy, come out here this minute! Sharon, Jerry, Loretta, where are you hiding?"

She started across the bridge. Then she thought she heard something like whispers in the wind. "Mother, don't come. Go back, Mother. Go back."

She stopped. She listened again. Now she heard nothing but the water flowing under the bridge. She looked down at it. It was green and glassy and it glistened as the sun shone down upon it.

If things were different, she would like to stay in just such a green forest spot as this, lean on that bridge and look down at that water a long time.

But she walked across the bridge, and she got so dizzy she had to hang onto the sides to keep from falling. She remembered she had eaten no breakfast. That was why she was dizzy.

She felt better when she looked up and saw the house. What a beautiful house! It was like a castle! With a stairway of broad stone steps going up to a big door. Where was she? Was this the Van Hummelwhite House, on the Canon Road? It must be. There was no house in town as big and beautiful. Still she was not sure. She didn't remember those stone steps. How had she gotten here? And if the children were here, what were they doing here?

She didn't know, but suddenly she began to feel better. The terrible feeling of fear she had known when she walked into their empty bedrooms this morning began to leave her. Mrs. Van Hummelwhite was a very nice person, and if the children were here, then it was mysterious, but it was all right.

She saw someone waving at her. It was a man in a military uniform with a sword at his side. He was coming down the stone steps and he was holding out his hand. Mother wished she had remembered to wear a nicer dress.

"Mrs. Mason, good morning," he cried out, "what a nice surprise."

Mother thought, "Do I know him? He knows me."

So she said, "How nice to see you, what a lovely morning."

He came on down the steps, crooking his arm for her to lean on.

"The Countess will be delighted. You must have strawberries and cream with us."

The Countess? This surprised Mother. So Mrs. Van

Hummelwhite was entertaining countesses these days. Still puzzled, she took the General's arm, however, and they walked up the steps.

"I'm looking for my children," she told him, still wondering who he was and how he knew her.

"How interesting!" He held the door open for her. "Do you do that sort of thing quite often?"

Then she was in a big beautiful room. She saw first a breakfast table in the center of the room and then, stepping out of the shadows, she saw a beautiful blond woman in ivory satin. When Mother first saw the beautiful woman she thought, "Oh, how beautiful she is." She next thought, "How shabby I am."

But the woman smiled at her so sweetly and suddenly she did not feel shabby. She felt beautiful and interesting and young and exciting.

"Mrs. Mason," the woman said, holding out a small white hand, "you didn't forget us. Thank you. Bless you." She led Mother to a chair.

Forget them? Then she must have met them. She wished she could remember where. But she must not offend them. So she said, "Forget you? How could I? How nice it is to be here." She looked at the table, set for breakfast and something odd ticked in her mind. Someone had been eating at this table. There was jelly dribbled across one of the plates. Jerry must not be the

only one who did that with grape jelly—held it high and always let it dribble down.

The man and woman were watching her. "Have I interrupted your breakfast?" she asked them. "Do go on."

The woman poured a cup of coffee from a silver pot and handed it to her.

"Thank you, but I do not have time for coffee. I'm looking for my children. Tell me, have you seen three children, or possibly—four?"

The General nodded. "Many times. And I have seen twenty children, fifty children, a hundred children. Once at a circus, I saw five hundred."

"You see." The Countess smiled at Mother. "He always tells more than is asked of him. Don't you adore him?"

Mother looked at him. No, she didn't adore him. He had given her a silly answer. She frowned. "I mean only my children. They are missing and I am out looking for them."

The General rose and bowed. "I imagine you do that as you do everything else—charmingly."

Mother was getting a little impatient with him. "Have you seen them?" she asked. "Have they been playing around here? They ran away last night." She was beginning to get frightened again. "Perhaps Mrs. Van Hummelwhite has seen them."

"Perhaps," said the Countess. "I expect she has seen

many things in her day. Do have some fresh strawberries."

Mother's voice was beginning to get tearful. "May I trouble you to speak to Mrs. Van Hummelwhite?"

"No trouble at all," the Countess smiled, "if she were here."

Mother was stunned. "But where is she?"

The Countess picked a rose out of a vase. "I wouldn't have the vaguest idea. General, do let me pin this flower in your buttonhole."

Mother was getting more and more impatient and frightened.

"Oh, do stop being so elegant and so charming, you two, and tell me. Have you seen my children, yes or no."

The Countess regarded her coldly, "My dear friend. Aren't you forgetting your manners?"

Mother's face got red. "I beg your pardon. I am so worried. But maybe you don't know how awful it is to run into their rooms to kiss your children and find—no one."

The Countess rose. "Stop," she cried. "This sentimental chatter bores me."

Mother started for the door. "I must go. I am wasting time here."

At the door she turned again and looked at the dribbled plate.

"A silly question," she said, "but I must ask it. Whoever did that jelly-dribbling on that plate?"

"Couldn't say," and here the General's eyes met those of the Countess. "We had guests for breakfast. I am not sure just which one of them was a jelly dribbler. Do you know, Countess?"

The Countess's voice was firm. "To the best of my knowledge I have never met a jelly dribbler. But then, maybe I did and was not aware of it at the time. One meets many types these days."

"Good-bye," said Mother. "I'm sorry I troubled you."

The General was opening the door for her when Mother heard the noise. It was the noise of feet, like squirrels, scampering under the floor. She heard some-one stumble and cry out.

Jerry! That was Jerry's voice coming from under the floor!

"Jerry!" she cried out. "Jerry, where are you?"

"Where is he?" She turned to the General, "I heard my little boy, Jerry. I know it."

The Countess held up her hand. "Yes, I heard some-thing, too. It came—from out there." She looked toward the forest.

Mother believed her. "Did it?" she cried. She ran to-ward the door. The Countess breathed a sigh of relief.

But as Mother walked again over that rug, she heard again under it the sound of scampering feet.

"I heard it again," she told them, "and it's coming from down there." She pointed to the floor.

"Of course you did," the General smiled. "Dear lady, you heard the noise of the Countess's pet monkeys in the cellar. Would you care to see them?"

"Another time, perhaps," said Mother. "But now I must look in that forest for my children. Good-bye and thank you."

As Mother started out the door for the third time, she heard Kathy's voice. It came from the floor under her feet. Suddenly her spine grew cold. She could not speak at first from fear. She looked at the General. His hand was on his sword. She looked at the Countess and the soft beautiful eyes were now like blue flames. Whoever they were, wherever she was, Mother knew now that these people had her children!

When she could speak, she tried to make her voice sound easy. But when she heard it, it sounded strange and dry and a little as though it belonged to someone else. She heard it say, "It's a lovely morning. A perfect morning for looking at pet monkeys. I believe I will see them after all."

"Certainly, Mrs. Mason." The Countess glared hatefully at Mother.

"Is this wise, my dear?" she heard the General whisper. But the Countess tossed her head.

"Wise or not, I will not be humiliated by this woman. Open the trap door."

With her heart beating, Mother saw the General lift a small rug off the floor and she saw a heavy iron ring. Just before he took hold of the ring to pull it up, the Countess said, "Wait!"

He stopped. She spoke to Mother.

"Mrs. Mason, do you love your home?"

"My home," said Mother. "Of course I love my home. I have a little green bedroom, high up under a chimney, with green leaves tapping at my window. I have a little china chandelier, made of pink and white flowers. In the dining room I have my grandmother's lace cloth. In the living room I have an oil painting of my father, a brick fireplace, a gold sofa with an ink stain. My home, I love every inch of the big rambling old place."

"Then think carefully," the Countess warned. "Once the General lifts this ring, you will never see your home again."

"Never see my home—" Well, Mother swallowed, but she thought of Kathy and Jerry and Sharon and Loretta and instantly made up her mind. If they lived in a boxcar, slept in hayfields, she would have her children.

"Lift the ring!" She threw up her head. And again the General touched the ring with his hand.

"Wait!" said the Countess. "There is someone else. Isn't there someone else across the bridge?"

Mother did not understand at first. Then she knew. She could read it in the Countess's eyes. Colin! Live without Colin! Colin live without her! Never!

The Countess was watching her. "I thought not," she said. "General, put back the rug. I think Mrs. Mason is leaving us after all."

Leaving? Leaving the children here! How would she explain this to Colin. "Colin, I have left your brother and sisters under a trap door to come back home to you." What would he think of her. No matter what he said, in his heart he would think, "Chicken! Cream puff! You left them, even the little ones, to come back here to me. Don't you know I could get along? I am the oldest. I am—a man. I can sell papers. I can work after school. I can grow up hard and tough. It will be lonely. It will be hard, but it will be better than sitting night after night in a warm dining room with a full meal with a mother who would go away and leave four children in a cellar under a rug."

"Oh, Colin," thought Mother, "you would be ashamed of a mother like that. And I would be ashamed of you if you weren't. So live, grow up, my boy, back there without us."

Mother turned to the Countess. "My son, Colin, would be ashamed of a cream puff for a mother. Lift up the ring."

The Countess was startled. She looked at the proud

lift of Mother's head. She raised a nervous hand to her pearl necklace.

"But surely, Mrs. Mason," she said, "surely a boy that age needs his mother."

Mother turned her head away so that the Countess should not see the tears in her eyes. When she spoke she was not like a countess. She was like a queen.

"I hardly think, Countess," she answered, "I want to discuss my son with you. And now if you don't mind will you open that trap door and bring my children up out of that cellar."

"Oh no, Madam," the General growled, "it is you who will go down."

"And then," said the Countess, "after we have chained you, we will bring your children up. And I shall have my heart's desire, children—forever."

The General took hold of Mother to put her down the cellar, when suddenly the Countess screamed. There was a huge finger pushing through the windows, moving blindly around, knocking over tables and chairs.

The General unsheathed his sword and rushed forward. "En garde!" he shouted, and plunged his sword into the finger.

Then they heard a bellowing voice outside, "Jeepers."

"Colin," Mother ran to the window and looked out. All she could see was an immense pair of legs in blue

jeans, like two telegraph poles. But it was Colin's voice!

The finger was still moving. It had now encircled the Countess by the waist and was pulling her out through the windows and up into the air!

Peering out of the window to look, Mother saw the giant now more clearly.

"Colin," she cried out. "Colin, what are you doing? How dare you swell up like that? Stop it, this instant! I'll spank you."

"See what a fine, big son I have," she turned to the General. "I don't know how he got that big—but he did it anyway. So I don't think you will put me in any cellar now."

"Not so quickly," growled the General, and he took her by the arm and pulled her outside.

She was suddenly frightened speechless. She felt a tickling at her throat. It was the point of the General's sword!

Colin was looking at the figure of the Countess. How small she was as she lay in a dead faint on the roof of the house in her ivory satin dress. She looked exactly like one of his sisters' dolls, lying on the roof of a dollhouse.

When Colin had run through the tunnel a few moments ago, he had started to run across the bridge. Then, with one foot on it, he had remembered the last thing Mrs. Newby had said to him. "Don't cross the bridge.

Walk upstream." So he had turned back.

At first he had seen nothing. Where was the house? What had happened?

Then he had looked down. There it lay. A dollhouse of a mansion with the broad stone steps no bigger than the width of his hand. Why, he could step over and kick it with his foot and it would tumble down.

Then he leaned over and tried to look in. He put his finger inside. When he pulled it out, there was the Countess. Now he heard a noise like flies buzzing.

There at the doorway of the house, he saw the General and his mother—his own mother—ten inches tall! The General had hold of her. He was shouting.

Colin reached down to pick him up. Then he heard his mother's voice—so small and birdlike, "Don't, Colin. Don't. Stop! Stop!"

"One move and I'll kill her." He heard the tiny, angry voice. The General had his sword at Mother's throat. Gosh!

"Hello, Colin," he heard a voice say close to his ears. He turned and saw Mrs. Newby standing there. He had an idea.

"I'll call a truce," he told her. "You go in and tell him I will give him back his Countess for my mother and brother and sisters."

Mrs. Newby was so pleased. "All my life I have wanted

to be inside of a dollhouse. Yes, I'll do your negotiating. How do I get in there?"

"The bridge," said Colin. And then Mrs. Newby walked to the bridge, disappeared for a moment behind the trees at the side of it. In a minute he saw her coming across the bridge. She was ten inches high.

So that was what happened! Something in the center of the bridge. He saw her go up to Mother and the General, and the three of them went inside the house. He looked at the Countess on the roof and waited.

Inside now, Mrs. Newby was facing the General, who still held Mother firmly, her arms behind her back, his sword unsheathed.

"Those are the terms," she told him. "All of the Masons for your countess."

"Done," said the general, and he let go of Mother. "But Colin hands down the Countess first. Then I open the door for all of you to return across the bridge. My word of honor."

Mother was worried. "How do we know we can trust you?"

"You don't." His lip curled. "You must take my word of honor, as a soldier and a gentleman."

"Well," said Mrs. Newby, "that has a nice sound to it. What do you think, Mrs. Mason?"

Mother looked at the iron ring on the floor and then at

the General's face. Both looked hard and cold.

"He may have a sense of honor," she decided. "Such things were fashionable once. We'll take the chance."

She ran outside and called up to Colin. "Colin, Colin." She cupped her hands around her mouth. "Put her down. Bring her back."

The Countess was coming to now and she stood upon the roof and stamped her tiny foot.

"Boor," she cried, "how dare you! Put me down—this instant."

Colin put his hand around her waist and gently lifted her off the roof. She squirmed and kicked like a small animal in his hand.

He sat her down at the top of the stone stairway. He saw her lift her head and sweep haughtily into the house, followed by Mother. Then he waited.

The Countess, as she passed Mother, said, "I will never forgive him, never, so it's no good your pleading for him."

The General hurried to her side. "Are you quite all right, my dear?" She nodded and walked to the fireplace to arrange her hair.

The General told her the agreement. She turned pale.

"Let them return! Now that they know? No one has ever learned our secret—and returned."

"I gave my word," he reminded her, "and my word is my life."

"Very well," she answered. "Let those who wish to go—go. Let those who wish to remain—remain."

The General took hold of the ring, pulled up the trap door, and the children, blinking from the darkness, climbed slowly up into the room. Jerry was first, then Sharon, then Kathy, and finally Loretta.

Jerry and Sharon and Kathy rushed to Mother and crowded around her like chicks around a hen. Loretta stood to one side, her face turned away.

"My darlings!" Mother hugged them so tight.

"Mother! Mother!" they cried out as they hugged her.

"Please," yawned the Countess, "do spare me this sentimental slush. I despise that word mother."

The children grew quiet. They did not look at the Countess now.

"Mother, we want to go home," they whispered.

"Come," and Mother took hold of Loretta's arm.

The Countess held her arms out to Loretta. "Loretta! Don't go. Not you. Don't leave me. Let me have one child of my own."

But Mother held Loretta. "Loretta, come with me."

"Why?" Loretta asked.

"Because I love you," said Mother.

"She loves me, too." Loretta pointed at the Countess. "And she will let me stay here and not send me back to the Pottses."

"That wicked creature," Mother looked at the Countess. "She stole you from me in the first place or you would never have left home at all. Yes, I understand it all now. And she has been trying to steal the others, too. It was not you, Loretta. It was she. Encouraging them to be naughty, just as she encouraged you. So please come with me now."

Now the Countess put her arms around Loretta.

"Don't go back over the bridge, dear child. Over there are many tears. Here there is always fun and laughter and music and dancing."

"Yes," Mother nodded, "there are tears over that bridge, but there are wonderful things, too. Remember, Loretta, how exciting it can be and how unexpected? Here everything is the same all the time. There, it is changing from sun to rain, rain to snow. One never knows what will happen next."

Loretta nodded. "Like the time Mr. Potts was hiding behind the door and popped me over the head with a rolled up *Saturday Evening Post*."

The Countess laughed. "Dear Loretta! She is never dull."

Loretta leaned against her. The Countess stroked her hair.

"I will stay with you always," she said, "and laugh and dance and listen to your music."

"She has made her choice." The Countess smiled.

"And now take your brood and go."

"No, no," Mother cried. "I love you, Loretta, please come home with me."

"We love you too, Loretta," cried Sharon and Jerry. "At first we didn't but now we do. Please come home with us."

"Please come home with us," said Kathy, "you are our very own big sister and I will let you play sometimes with Irene Irene Lavene."

Then she remembered. "Irene Irene!" and Kathy ran to the window and looked out at the bridge. "She's gone. She's gone. Where's Irene?"

Loretta ran to the window. "She's gone. Where is Irene Irene, Countess?"

The Countess was embarrassed. "I could not help it. I had to dispose of her. She was blocking our bridge. We set fire to her last night and swept the ashes into the stream this morning."

Before anyone could stop her, Loretta let out a cry of rage and made a grab for the Countess's hair. The Countess screamed but Loretta's hands were yanking her yellow curls and Loretta was screaming, "You burned Irene. You burned Irene. I hate you!"

"Help," cried the Countess to Mother. "Take her. Stop her. She's your child."

Mother had to take Loretta's arms and fasten them behind her back as she smiled at the Countess. "Loretta is never dull—remember?"

Then Mother pulled her to the door and Jerry and Sharon and Kathy followed.

There was a piercing sad cry from the Countess.

"Children! Children! Oh, why do you always leave me?" And she turned away her beautiful face and laid it on her arms in grief. The General bowed his head, in shame, and his sword hung limply from his side.

How sad and lonely they both looked!

No one said a word as they tiptoed out and hurried over the bridge as fast as they could.

For one second they all stood by the bank of the stream and looked across.

There it lay, dreaming in the sunlight, the little castle with the stone staircase, the little stone chimneys and the tiny door with the iron knocker in the shape of a lion's head.

It *was* a dear little thing!

From the bottom of the hill there came the sound of the cows mooing on the Potts farm.

The children said nothing. They knew they would never see the little castle again. Only Mrs. Newby spoke.

"If they had asked me to stay, I would have," she sighed. "All my life I have wanted to live in a dollhouse."

When they got back into the house again, Mother called the carpenter before she took off her hat.

"Come and board up a wall with strong wooden beams so nobody can ever get through it again."

Loretta was still crying. But she said nothing at all as the carpenter came and put nails into boards at the back of the closet.

Kathy looked at Irene Irene Lavene's little chair.

"Once, I had the most beautiful doll in the whole world."

"Me, too," said Loretta. "She was mine, too."

"She wasn't," said Kathy.

"She's gone forever," said Loretta. "And so she can be mine, too."

"Loretta is right," said Mother. "And it is sad about Irene Irene Lavene. But we had to pay for all of this some way. And we are all safe and we are all home. So let's be thankful."

Kathy said, "We will put a wreath of flowers on her little rocking chair and nobody will ever sit in that chair again."

Loretta and Kathy and Jerry and Sharon went out to get the flowers. But Colin stayed in the room and watched his mother as she went about the house singing and straightening things up. There was something he could not understand and would never understand.

Back there when he was so big and she was so small, he could have broken her in two with one hand. Yet, when she called him, his neck got hot and that same feeling came into the pit of his stomach. Size, he decided, had nothing to do with any of it.

And just to be sure, Mother often went into Kathy's old room—Loretta's room—and looked at the boards at the back of the closet. Once she held her ear down close to the wall and thought to herself, maybe it was all a dream anyway. But soon she jumped back. There was the faint sound of an orchestra playing dance music.

The Countess was giving a party over there!

Mother never listened at that wall again!

MARY COYLE CHASE (1907–1981) was born in Denver, Colorado, and lived there all her life. She worked for various Denver papers as a journalist, began to write plays, and in 1944 had a huge success with *Harvey*, which won the Pulitzer Prize and was later made into a movie starring Jimmy Stewart.

HAROLD BERSON (1926–1986) was born in Los Angeles and studied art in Paris. *Loretta Mason Potts*, originally published in 1958, was the first book he illustrated, but he would go on to draw pictures for more than ninety books, including many that he also wrote.

SELECTED TITLES IN THE
NEW YORK REVIEW CHILDREN'S COLLECTION

ESTHER AVERILL
Captains of the City Streets
The Hotel Cat
Jenny and the Cat Club
Jenny Goes to Sea
Jenny's Birthday Book
Jenny's Moonlight Adventure
The School for Cats

JAMES CLOYD BOWMAN
Pecos Bill: The Greatest Cowboy of All Time

PALMER BROWN
Beyond the Pawpaw Trees
Cheerful
Hickory
The Silver Nutmeg
Something for Christmas

SHEILA BURNFORD
Bel Ria: Dog of War

DINO BUZZATI
The Bears' Famous Invasion of Sicily

MARY CHASE
Loretta Mason Potts

CARLO COLLODI and FULVIO TESTA
Pinocchio

INGRI and EDGAR PARIN D'AULAIRE
D'Aulaires' Book of Animals
D'Aulaires' Book of Norse Myths
D'Aulaires' Book of Trolls
Foxie: The Singing Dog
The Terrible Troll-Bird
Too Big
The Two Cars

EILÍS DILLON
The Island of Horses
The Lost Island

ELEANOR FARJEON
The Little Bookroom

PENELOPE FARMER
Charlotte Sometimes

PAUL GALLICO
The Abandoned

LEON GARFIELD
The Complete Bostock and Harris
Smith: The Story of a Pickpocket

RUMER GODDEN
An Episode of Sparrows
The Mousewife

MARIA GRIPE and HARALD GRIPE
The Glassblower's Children

LUCRETIA P. HALE
The Peterkin Papers

RUSSELL and LILLIAN HOBAN
The Sorely Trying Day

RUTH KRAUSS and MARC SIMONT
The Backward Day

DOROTHY KUNHARDT
Junket Is Nice
Now Open the Box

MUNRO LEAF and ROBERT LAWSON
Wee Gillis

RHODA LEVINE and EDWARD GOREY
He Was There from the Day We Moved In
Three Ladies Beside the Sea

BETTY JEAN LIFTON and EIKOH HOSOE
Taka-chan and I

NORMAN LINDSAY
The Magic Pudding

ERIC LINKLATER
The Wind on the Moon

J. P. MARTIN
Uncle
Uncle Cleans Up

JOHN MASEFIELD
The Box of Delights
The Midnight Folk

WILLIAM McCLEERY and WARREN CHAPPELL
Wolf Story

JEAN MERRIL and RONNI SOLBERT
The Pushcart War

E. NESBIT
The House of Arden

ALFRED OLLIVANT's
Bob, Son of Battle: The Last Gray Dog of Kenmuir
A New Version by LYDIA DAVIS

DANIEL PINKWATER
Lizard Music

ALASTAIR REID and BOB GILL
Supposing...

ALASTAIR REID and BEN SHAHN
Ounce Dice Trice

BARBARA SLEIGH
Carbonel and Calidor
Carbonel: The King of the Cats
The Kingdom of Carbonel

E. C. SPYKMAN
Terrible, Horrible Edie

FRANK TASHLIN
The Bear That Wasn't

VAL TEAL and ROBERT LAWSON
The Little Woman Wanted Noise

JAMES THURBER
The 13 Clocks
The Wonderful O

ALISON UTTLEY
A Traveller in Time

T. H. WHITE
Mistress Masham's Repose

MARJORIE WINSLOW and ERIK BLEGVAD
Mud Pies and Other Recipes

REINER ZIMNIK
The Bear and the People